"DON'T SAY GOOD NIGHT YET!"

whispered Sarah, the untamed girl of
the swamps.

They were alone in Dave's room after he had
brutally whipped the leader of the river pirates.

That afternoon hot-blooded Dave had thought
her the most desirable woman he'd ever
seen. But tonight he knew she belonged to
these vicious outlaws—who might discover
at any moment the real reason why he
had invaded their evil hideout.

"You shouldn't be here," he said, as she
approached the bed. "You're only a girl."

"I don't know where else I'd be," was her
frank reply. "You won me, didn't you?"

A NOVEL OF THE AMERICAN FRONTIER

THE WILD YEARS

DONN O'HARA

WILDSIDE PRESS

CHAPTER 1

ISLANDS crowded each other like swimmers in an up-stream race, all along this stretch of river. Then too, the boat had to navigate around the usual tricky snags which cluttered the channel. So naturally the men in the smoking cabin thought nothing of it when, for the first time since Vicksburg, the *Tuscaloosa* cut her speed so drastically that they could not feel the throb of her engines. Almost any other boat would have been tied up under some convenient bank since nightfall. The *Tuscaloosa*, a river queen with a crack pilot, could steam onward through the darkness, but it only stood to reason that she'd change pace now and then.

Young David Macdonough paid no attention to the boat's behavior. He was too busy measuring his gambling companions.

There were nine men in the cabin, including the bartender, who kept his eye on the game even while he fetched drinks. The action was fast enough to suit anybody. Two players had been cleaned out, but they could not or would not leave. The play fascinated them still.

The trouble was, David Macdonough confessed to himself, it looked as if he would soon join the two losers at just being fascinated. He was down to his last twenty and he didn't own a damned thing on which to raise a stake. He fingered the chain looped across his red-shot-with-silver waistcoat, and clucked regretfully. If only a good watch nestled in the pocket at the end of the chain . . . but the devil with wishing. He had a steady hand, a long panatela to light up for show, and strong nerves to hang on until something broke his way. If it did break his way.

Maybe this time, he thought. He'd held worse cards. "That," he said firmly, and enriched the pot.

Three dropped, but two called. The two who called were formidable, each riding a winning streak. Judge Ryerson was a planter, fabulously wealthy, petulant, im-

5

petuous. Martineau was squat, suave, unsmiling, a watchful man despite his heavy lids. Martineau somehow suggested a tired bishop, but he owned great gobs of New Orleans—including quite a few planks in this vessel, the *Tuscaloosa*.

"Something tells me I'm it," the judge said on a rising note. "I've got whores."

Martineau sighed. "Beats my jay-boys," he admitted, and threw in his hand.

"Bullets," David said. He felt his insides relax as if that last shot of mellow bourbon actually had taken hold for a change. He showed his cards and reached for the pot.

And then someone said, "Oh, my God."

David hadn't heard the door open, and neither had anyone else. Midnight lay behind them. No singing rose from the boiler deck. The dancers had long since deserted the ballroom, and the boat's engines must have been shut off entirely, for she seemed to drift idly in time and space. And yet the players had not looked up, so absorbed were they in the game. Nobody had seen or heard the three men until this moment.

The bartender must have let out that yawp, David reflected, and his insides went tight again as he studied the river pirates.

The three men wore linsey-woolsey, shaggy shapeless suits of no definite color. Their moccasins were muddy. The brims of their black hats flopped down over their faces—but the faces couldn't be seen anyway, because black cotton masks covered them.

Two pirates, armed with rifles, stood in the doorway. The third held a naked knife. He crouched low as he worked, but he must have been a tall man; his shoulders seemed enormous, and Dave deduced from the movements of the mask that it contained a lot of whiskers.

"Back to the wall," the knife man said. "Anybody goes for a gun, he gits kilt."

Approximately one hundred dollars in cash formed a beautifully untidy heap on the table. The crouching knife man swept it all up, stuffed it into a canvas bag suspended from his neck, and went on with his collection. He took watches, chains and wallets. He didn't bother with rings, but he patted under arms and around waists to check for money belts. He found one, and the subsequent partial disrobing impressed David as being so comical that he almost grinned.

6

Then the collector came to him, and it wasn't funny at all. The man pulled out his wallet, looked inside, grunted in disgust and threw the wallet down. He yanked at David's watch chain, and when it came away with absolutely nothing at the end of it, David couldn't maintain his poker face.

"Sorry," he told the man lightly, but he knew he was blushing.

"Always one in every crowd," the man muttered, and turned away.

It had been fast, very fast. The crouching man, having frisked each player, nipped behind the bar, snatched up a huge tarantula pistol, dropped this too into his canvas bag, and was gone. The two riflemen stepped back onto the deck. The door slammed, and that ended it, so far as the cabin was concerned. David eyed his panatela. Practically no ash at all, it had happened so quickly.

The thing seemed incredible, really. This year of Our Lord, 1848, had been a profitable one for river pirates, and like everyone else, David knew that they favored this very stretch, the swampland between the river and the old Natchez Trace. Here, obviously, they could ply their trade with the greatest margin of safety, making their raids, and then when pursuit got hot, disappearing among the wooded islands that made up Satan's Brood. But, by God, there were river pirates and river pirates!

Those three had been contemptible cutthroats, the kind who would swarm over a flatboat, slaughtering the whole family for the sake of pots and pans and a few bales of pelts. That such trash should strike at a boat like the *Tuscaloosa*—well, it gave a man something to think about.

David puffed his panatela and thought a lot about it in the space of seconds, while he watched the other eight men out of the corner of his eye. They had reacted as he expected, showing shock, anger, and bewilderment all at once. Even now they just stood there, baffled, probably supposing that the visitors had been deck passengers from below, riffraff on a rampage.

Judge Ryerson was the first to move. With a roar of rage he sprang to the door and flung it open. Beyond the judge, David saw the narrow strip of promenade deck, and the rail, and the after part of the larboard paddle-house. Beyond that, and below, was the river, black as pitch.

David said, "Judge—"

7

The judge teetered in the doorway, perfectly silhouetted. There were two sharp cracks, as if somebody had slapped boards together, and two spurts of orange flame. Something skittered across the ceiling and thumped into the far wall. Splinters dribbled down from the groove it had made.

"Duck!" David yelled, and leaped at Ryerson. He got a hand on the judge's collar and yanked hard, downward. The judge resisted, stunned into idiocy, and David put a foot into the back of his knee. A push with the foot, another yank on the collar, and the judge came down. He landed with a thump, sat up groggily, and looked at the ceiling. He saw the groove the ball had dug, and he looked out of the door again.

"That came from a boat," he whispered as if he had uncovered a great truth. "It was a real holdup—I've got to see after Ella!"

He scrambled up, wheezing, bolted through the doorway and ran to the right, doubled over as he pounded along the dark deck. David heard no shots, and when he peeped outside he saw that the *Tuscaloosa*, ravished, all white, was floating free. No moon hung above, no stars. So few lights did the silent boat show that David couldn't tell where water left off and sky began. The shore on both sides seemed but a vague blur.

One by one the others followed the judge, each seeking to determine the safety of a wife or some other female relative, not to mention certain valuable articles left in the stateroom. Only David Macdonough remained in the smoking cabin. He had no wife. He had a stateroom with precisely nothing of value in it. He tucked the ends of his watch chain back into the lower waistcoat pockets, and he sat down again, staring glumly at the place on the table where the cash had lain.

One by one they came back. Others came, too—the captain and the supercargo. There was a swirl of indignant talk, out of which a story gradually emerged. David Macdonough listened quietly.

There had been at least eight men, all masked. They had boarded the boat unseen, just at the moment when the *Tuscaloosa* came almost to a stop at one of the sharpest and narrowest of the channel twists. They had not tampered with the machinery, but pointed a gun at the second engineer, the officer in charge of the boiler deck, and ordered him to keep everything just as it was.

Four of them went on to the supercargo's room, clearly marked, and hauled him out of his bunk, forcing him to show them the safe. And then they carried the safe away —literally carried it.

Three others had entered the smoking saloon, but none had gone up to the texas, where Eb Sterns, the pilot, stood insulated in his glass house. Eb would never have known that anything had gone wrong if he hadn't rung his bells and received no response. Finally suspicious at that point, he sent his cub below to find out what in thunderation they were doing down there, and the boy, encountering one of the masked men in a corridor, had been badly cudgeled.

This, however, was the only casualty. The whole business had been timed and carried out with the precision of a drill. The shots fired at Judge Ryerson had doubtless been intended only as a warning. In themselves they had caused no disturbance. Many, asleep, never heard them. Others might have been awakened, but attached no importance to the sounds. Hands and passengers often fired at bits of floating refuse, and it was a common practice, when any boat such as the *Tuscaloosa* approached or passed some small landing place, for the watchers there to let off a few bangs out of sheer exuberance.

The *Tuscaloosa* carried almost a hundred cabin class travelers, in addition to the deck passengers, and it seemed likely that not a single one, other than the gamblers in the smoking saloon, knew that anything untoward had occurred.

Out of this clatter of talk, indignation and demands that something be done—out of the jerky and sometimes foolish things said by reason of suddenly released nerves —there gradually emerged an estimate of the loss, as well as the sobering realization of what this meant. These were steamboat men, all interested, directly or otherwise, in river traffic. They knew it would be impossible to keep the news of this lightning raid quiet. The deed, so successful, would be imitated again and again. As insurance rates soared it would be necessary to hire armed guards, which in turn would increase freight and passenger rates. Boats would have to avoid certain dangerous stretches after nightfall, thus disrupting schedules at a time when competition was fierce and everything depended on speed.

David Macdonough sat silent, smoking and listening.

9

They went on and on, those rich men, moaning and re-peating the details of how they must do it the hard, the expensive way. For some reason he was reminded of the old saw anent the strong taking from the weak, and the smart taking from the strong. It didn't fit exactly, though. These men were strong, but not really stupid. The pirates were strong, but not actually . . . No, that didn't ring true, either. In this stretch of river, the pirates had the strength and the smartness as well. It all boiled down to knowing the local ground rules. These men knew the rules, and the tricks as well, in their counting-house world. The pirates knew the rules and tricks of their world. Who could take from the strong, the very smart pirates, then?

Another pirate, David Macdonough thought, and sat up straight.

They had begun to talk about the safe again. The pirates had taken a safe that contained $1,200. The poker losses came next, and the rich men were bemoaning the theft of their watches. David smiled secretly. He had no riches and he had no watch, and all he could cavil about was the outrage of interrupted privacy. If you couldn't have privacy in a poker game, then where on earth could you have it?

Nowhere, probably.

Not even a pirate could count on privacy . . . from other pirates.

"How much did you lose?" someone asked suddenly.

"I?" David cleared his threat. Was it possible that they had not seen that he owned no watch to offer those pirates? Yes, it was quite possible. Things had happened so fast. Even the pirates had been in such a hurry that they probably couldn't remember a single face in this cabin. "I?" he repeated. "Why, not much. Just all I had."

Judge Ryerson swore. "By God," he said, "I'd give a thousand dollars to get my watch back."

David took his cigar out of his mouth and started to say something. He changed his mind and put the cigar back again. A thousand dollars for the return of one watch, with so much more at stake? The idea grew and grew.

"I have influence in Baton Rouge," Ryerson was trumpeting. "And believe me, gentlemen, I intend to use it!"

"Place ain't in Louisiana," someone objected. "It's in Mississippi."

10

"Well, I got influence in Jackson too. And Washington. By God, I'll have federal marshals scouring that bank out there inside of a month."

Then Dave Macdonough did speak up.

"That won't do any good," he said. "They're alligator men. They would fade back into the swamp. Might get one or two, but that's all, Judge."

Suddenly they were all looking at him. No watch, he thought. No wife and no riches. Nothing but an idea and an opportunity to catch hold of. What have I got to lose except my fool life?

"Well," Martineau prompted, "what would *you* do, young man?"

David took it slowly, deliberately, gambler fashion. "The politicians have a saying, gentlemen: 'If you can't lick 'em, join 'em.' " He studied the smoke from his panatela. "It just happens that I'm out of a job right now, and I also have a plan in my mind for breaking up that gang and getting all of the loot back."

They stared at him. He stared back.

"Do you think," he said, "that you could raise ten thousand dollars for that, Mr. Martineau?"

"No trouble at all," Jason Martineau replied so easily that David almost blinked. "We'd have to have some kind of guarantee, of course."

"I wouldn't ask for anything until I came back," David told him. He stifled the temptation to add, "If I come back," and went on. "All I need in advance is perhaps fifty dollars for expenses."

Martineau frowned at him, narrow-eyed. Ryerson leaned forward and said, "That wouldn't buy you much gunpowder, young fellow. Or even—"

"I won't be using gunpowder," David said, fast, because fast was the only way he could get it out. "I won't carry a gun. Not even a knife."

They kept examining him as if he were a candidate for a lunatic asylum. He smiled serenely, to prove he wasn't. To prove to *them* that he wasn't.

"What about your men?" Martineau asked finally.

"No men," David said. "I'm going to do this job alone."

Judge Ryerson broke the silence. He said, "Young man, who are you, anyway? Where do you come from?"

"That's what I don't like about this country out here," David told him severely. "Wherever a man goes, somebody is sure to ask him that question. I reckon I'll have

11

to keep moving until I find a place where folks aren't so curious. Then, maybe, I'll settle down. But meanwhile, if you gentlemen are interested—and you do seem to be mighty interested—I've got a proposition for you."

Nobody said anything, so he waggled the panatela as if he were a schoolmarm shaking a footrule. "It's got to be understood that if I do this, it must be done on a no-questions-asked basis. Agreed?"

They all bobbed their heads at him.

"Good," he said briskly. "Now here's the plan."

Then he made up the rest of it as he talked. It came easy. As smooth and easy, it occurred to him in mid-harangue, as the glide of a river pirate's blade across an unarmed visitor's throat.

CHAPTER 2

THE GARDEN was flecked with fireflies. The air smelled of jasmine, a night bloomer in New Orleans, and of Cherokee roses. A hedge of hibiscus, its salmon-colored flowers gleaming through the darkness, lined the high iron fence. And from beyond the fence, from the street, where the coachmen and footmen and other servants waited, came handclapping, stomping, the shuffle of bare feet, and laughter. Rectangles of light lay on the grass, hurled there from windows, and across these swung the shadows of the dancers indoors.

A tall, grave young man stood beside an azalea. He wore somber clothes, and his head turned slowly, so that he regarded first the hedge, and then the fence, and then the windows.

He must be from out of town, Adoree thought, for she had never seen him before. He was not a guest. He might have come out of the library, a door of which opened upon the garden. Uncle Jason Martineau was forever holding small private conferences on business matters in his library. He held them even while his wife and daughters were entertaining.

Adoree had come out here to be alone. Still, she smiled at the stranger.

"You like to look both ways," she said, "like Janus?"

The young man raised his head slowly. He had large brown eyes, and even in that light Adoree could see a faint wash of freckles across his nose, a slightly uptilted nose which softened the seriousness of the brown eyes. He waited a moment before he spoke.

"Yes," he said, and she knew right-off that he was a Yankee. "The two worlds—I always admire to see 'em side by side, and hear 'em too. I travel the river, ma'am, and I like to stand at the stern end of the promenade at night and look down at the boiler deck. I take in the machinery, and all the glare from the fires, and the whisky barrel, and the deck passengers lying every-which-way or else maybe dancing or singing. And then all around me, up where I stand, there's classical music, and beautiful ladies in silk, and gentlemen with diamond studs." He grinned. "I like it."

"La, sir, you prate like a poet!"

She regretted that cry even as she made it. She sounded not saucy, but simply silly, affected.

"All the same, sir," she added in haste, "I'll warrant that you're glad to be on that upper deck looking *down* rather than on the boiler deck looking *up*."

"I've been on the boiler deck too," he said.

The waltz ended and Adoree heard the customary clitter-clatter of talk, the clipped polite clapping. Out in the garden it sounded hot and thin, like potatoes frying on a stove. Shadows no longer wheeled across the parallelograms of light. From the other side of the hedge the people who couldn't be seen had struck up another song.

"Stagolee, Stagolee, what's dat in you' grip?"
"Nothin' but my Sunday clothes,
I'm going to take a trip.
"Oh, dat man, bad man, Stagolee done come."

Adoree went to the stranger, holding out her hand. After all, she was a sort of secondary hostess here.

"I am Adoree Sanderson," she said. "Mrs. Martineau's neice."

"Pleased to meet you. Name's Macdonough."

He simply took her hand and shook it. He did not kiss it or even bow over it. His own hand felt cool, but dry, not clammy.

Now that her eyes had begun to adjust to the darkness, she could make out this man better. He was tall, and there was something very firm about him. He looked as if he'd be hard to rock, even to budge. Oh, he was a

13

Yank all right, and made no bones about it; yet his nails seemed clean, and his neck too. His frockcoat was high-waisted, very full in the skirt, modish but not foppish, its color a conventional bottle-green. His waistcoat was of velvet or perhaps velveteen, maroon silvered with fleurs-de-lis, and he wore a watch chain across it. His trousers, hitched high, were probably stockinet. His face was hairless, his head hatless.

"You say you travel the river, Mr. Macdonough? What do you do, if it's not too bold asking? I'm interested because I am going to take a river trip myself in a few days."

"I'm a gambler, ma'am. A professional gambler."

Adoree gasped. The gambling gentry had been the curse of river travel ever since the invention of the steamboat. Lately there had been a drive to exterminate them. They hurt business. The trapper who had lost in two hours the savings of two hard lonesome years, the salesman who watched his firm's money as well as his own go down before marked cards, were not, in their understandable bitterness, good advertisements for steamboating. Some skippers, alas, split with the gamblers. Others would have no part of them.

It was difficult to catch a gambler in the act of cheating, and still more difficult to know what to do with him when you did. Steamers operating in a navigable stream were, when not tied up, technically within federal jurisdiction; but the power of Washington was weak in these parts. A game started while the boat was moored somewhere in Louisiana, might not end until Mississippi or even Tennessee or Missouri. Had a crime been committed? and if so, had it been continuous or a single act? And if a single act, where had it taken place? To put an offender ashore at the nearest town or city and cause his arrest, meant leaving one or two officers of the boat with him in order to press charges, an awkward and expensive procedure; and then the scoundrel, having money and a smart lawyer, probably would go scot-free.

Gambling was not a new problem. The only thing new about it was the way certain skippers had begun to solve it. When they learned that a professional gamester had eluded their watchfulness in port and was operating at the expense of the passengers, they simply put him ashore, no matter what his ticket said, no matter where the boat happened to be. This constituted a public dec-

14

laration of the boat's war on gamblers, and it had the added advantage of shaming the fellow publicly, giving all the passengers a chance to see him and avoid him later. Such marooning was, of course, strictly illegal. The gambler, when he found his way back to civilization, was entitled to sue for breach of contract, a ticket being a contract. But he seldom did. Operators of that sort preferred to stay as far away from the law as possible.

In the circumstances, then, it was breath-taking to hear a man identify himself as a professional river gambler. For an instant Adoree wondered if she'd just received a sample of that dry droll Yankee humor one heard about. But the man had no expression. He seemed to feel that he had closed the subject. He didn't show nervousness, or offer to chat about something else. He simply stood there.

She gave a guarded laugh.

"Could it be that I'm addressing the great Captain Flambeau himself?"

David shook his head.

"No, ma'am. Captain Flambeau—if he really exists— is a success. I happen to be a failure. I've tried it for the better part of a year now and I just can't seem to make gambling pay."

"Why, you poor man! Could it be that you aren't using the right tools?"

She felt a bit daring as she said this. Sometimes, out of sheer boredom, Adoree Sanderson insulted men she knew in New Orleans, where her beauty and her family protected her, but she had never tried this on a Yankee. Mr. Macdonough took it seriously, however.

"No, ma'am. I don't use tools and I don't have a capper —that's a partner. I just try to play better cards than the rest. But even then I can't seem to win. Leastways, not enough to make it pay."

"I see." Suddenly she was embarrassed. She shifted the talk. "You said *if* there was such a man as Captain Flambeau. You don't mean you never met up with that wonderworker in your travels?"

"No, ma'am, I never did. What's more, I never met anybody who *had*. Not anybody reliable, that is. Of course, it *could* be there's such a man. They sure tell a heap of stories about him."

"It sounds almost atheistic, not to believe in Flambeau."

15

"I don't mean it to be. Maybe Captain Flambeau does exist. Maybe he's even all they say. But I think he must be dead."

"Dead?"

"I figure there must have been *somebody* like that, to get the stories started. Seems as if folks just think they have to have some kind of a hero. Maybe they never did think of Captain Flambeau as a real man. If he hadn't been there they'd've invented him anyway."

"I see what you mean."

"I guess men like that don't live long, especially out this way. Where I come from they have a saying that what's got over the Devil's back must be spent under his belly."

Adoree was shocked: men had been called out to the field of honor for using words like that in the presence of a lady. But she smiled.

"And where *do* you come from, Mr. Macdonough?"

The music started up, another sugary waltz. Again the dancing shadows shuttled. Beyond the hedge, the men and boys were chanting:

> *"Stagolee start out, he give his wife his han':*
> *" 'Goodbye, darlin', I'm going to kill a man.'*
> *"Oh, dat man, bad man, Stagolee done come."*

About their feet the fireflies thickened. The stars hung clear and clean in a sky without moon. Finally David Macdonough spoke.

"You said you were going to make a boat trip soon?"

"Yes. Day after tomorrow. On the *Tuscaloosa*."

"Oh."

"Why?"

"I hate to hear it, that's all. I sure hate to hear it."

Adoree bridled. "Now see here, sir, couldn't you tell—"

"It's getting sort of chilly, ma'am, and the music's going again. Maybe I'd better take you back to the house."

She looked at him. She had never seen a more serious, preoccupied expression on any human face.

"Thank you," she said, and they went toward the house.

CHAPTER 3

IT seemed unlikely that so splendid a steamer as the *Tuscaloosa* would ever have to sail with empty staterooms, but it was an added proof of her fame that the raid at Satan's Brood had not cost her a single cancellation. She started her upriver trip packed to capacity, and the passengers expressed confidence in her skipper, the bouncy, belligerent, bewhiskered John Wells, a part owner of the boat he commanded, and Eb Sterns, whom many called the best pilot on the lower river.

Once aboard the passengers talked of little but the holdup. Some averred that they wouldn't get a wink of sleep the second night out, when the boat was due to pass the islands between Natchez and Vicksburg. Whether this loss of sleep was to be the result of timorousness or a wish to be in on whatever might happen, the speaker in each case suffered disappointment. A bit of trouble with the machinery, a slight delay here, another there, and high water for this time of the year, combined to make the *Tuscaloosa* fall behind schedule. She would not enter Satan's Brood until the morning of the third day.

"You must point this place out to me," Adoree Sanderson said to David Macdonough.

They both felt shy, embarrassed. The two nights had been wonderful. Neither could forget the nights, or even think of anything else. But here in the blaze of the texas, with nothing but cerulean sky above, a sky splotched with preposterously small white clouds, and the river rolling free, it seemed advisable to talk rather of the weather, or the rise, or the shore. They didn't look at one another.

"Satan's Brood?" David said. "We're coming to it right now."

She shaded her eyes. "It doesn't *look* sinister."

"It isn't. It's mostly mud."

"It looks like nothing at all. Just as if the river ended there."

"You can't see the channel yet. You'll hardly be able to see it even when we go into it, for that matter. It gives you a creepy feeling. It's like steaming straight into solid land. You wait for the bump—but it doesn't come."

17

"It's over on the right there?"

"Yes."

She reconnoitered him with a glance. He should have been bending over her, all eyes. She wore her new mantelet ruched with guipure and her open straw bonnet á *la Clarissa Harlowe;* she had never looked lovelier, and she knew it. But David stared straight ahead, the skin of his cheek very tight.

His face frightened her as much as it attracted her. Surely he had shaved only a little while ago, yet the beard showed blue at the jaw. The eyes were opened wide, as always. David never smiled—at least she had never seen him smile—he would sometimes grin; and when he grinned it was with his whole face, the eyes shutting, the mouth stretching very wide, while waxy yellow freckles all but leaped right out of the nose in which they had been imbedded.

"Well, I'm looking forward to it," she said. "*You* don't seem to be."

"I'm not," he said gravely.

"What's the matter?" she teased. "Afraid?"

Instantly, she rebuked herself. The airy nothingness, the raillery, the grace notes, as it were, of conversation —these had become a bad habit.

"Yes," he said. "Yes, I am afraid."

The statement startled and confused Adoree. She said, "Afraid—of another holdup, in broad daylight?"

"Oh, no, not that. That didn't amount to much anyway. It was over almost before we knew what had happened."

"*We?*"

She sat upright. She took his arm.

"David Macdonough, do you mean to tell me that you were here at the time of the holdup?"

"Well, not right here. I was back in the smoking saloon." And he added, "Practicing my profession."

"That sounds bitter."

"It wasn't meant to be. I've got nothing against gentlemen, not any more'n I have against ladies. I can understand how they feel, I guess."

"I know! That was why you were at Uncle Jason's the other night, the time I ran into you in the garden! It was a reunion!"

"Well, sort of. It started with that anyway. We—they were having a little conference, and they asked me to step outside a minute, which I did."

18

"A conference?" Adoree brightened. "You know, I never did believe you when you said you were a common river gambler. Uncle Jason wouldn't have anything to do with one of them. He certainly wouldn't invite one to his house."

"I never said I was a common river gambler. If you ask me, I'm a mighty *un*common one."

"I don't think you're a gambler at all."

He shrugged.

She regarded him a moment. She seemed about to say something, but suddenly she sank back.

"I don't know what we're talking about this for anyway," she murmured.

"I don't either," David said drearily.

"We should be talking about *us*, after last night."

Immediately she blushed. She was not an easy blusher; indeed, she rather despised females who used a rush of blood to the face as readily as they'd use a flirted fan or downcast eyes. It was a trick, nothing more. But now, here on the *Tuscaloosa's* texas, Adoree really did blush. She felt her whole face flame, and she turned her head away.

To make it worse, passengers were coming up from breakfast in increasing numbers, favoring the forward end of the texas, the highest deck, on one side or other of the pilot house. The attraction, to be sure, was not this pair but the approaching tangle of islands and mud-flats known as Satan's Brood. The place had always borne an evil name, and now the holdup had added to it the fascination that hovers over the scene of a crime. People wanted to stare at it—even though there was nothing much to see—precisely as people will stare at an empty stretch of sidewalk where a little earlier somebody had been shot, or gawk at a tree branch from which not long ago somebody had been lynched, though these may not differ remarkably from any other branch or stretch of sidewalk. The rail to right and left of Adoree and David was getting crowded. They had to hold their voices low.

"I shouldn't have kissed you," he said glumly.

"Why not? I let you."

"I still shouldn't have done it."

Her face under control now, her chin low, she peered at him from under the brim of her bonnet. He kept on staring straight ahead.

What a strange young man!

19

Adoree was used to evasions, highflown compliments, protestations, glittering bits and pieces of formal politeness, speeches that you delivered because you had learned them, without any regard for the meaning of the words themselves, as you might have learned to recite a poem in a foreign tongue. When David said something he meant it. You didn't have to rearrange it, check its pattern, look it up in a code book.

In her world you judged a man by his clothes, at least until you had something better to go by. David Macdonough's clothes were good, but they were not elegant, not rich. He would not have worn diamonds even if he could afford them. The most notable thing · about his apparel was its *tidiness*, just as the most notable feature of the man himself, his appearance that is, was his *cleanness*. He might not have been fastidious in the worldly, la-di-da sense of that word; but he looked scrubbed. He shone.

She said, "You owe me an explanation, I think."

"Can't see why any man should have to explain why he made love to a beautiful woman, if he got a chance."

Coming from Dave, this stunned her. A minute passed before she could answer. She leaned close, hitching her shoulders, giving him an excuse to readjust her mantelet if he wanted to. He didn't move.

Finally she whispered, "It isn't that you made love to me. It's that you stopped making love to me."

"Shouldn't have started in the first place," he said. "Shouldn't have come aboard this boat when I knew you were a passenger."

"In heaven's name, *why?*"

"You'll see," he promised, "in just a little while."

Now the steamboat went in among the islands. It was, as Dave had said, like entering solid shore. The channel was visible only to the trained eye of Eb Sterns.

Speed had been reduced. Steam shrieked through the 'scape pipes. But when this sound ceased, leaving no echoes, the silence was so eerie, it fairly tingled. The excitement of those who lined the rail was suppressed. When they spoke at all, they whispered. Indeed, any speech came hard in that wet choky air.

It was like going up a watery corridor, a tunnel. In places even the sunlight failed to crash through the overhang, so that everything became dim, dank. Cypress and live-oak actually brushed the *Tuscaloosa* as she slid by

20

at quarter-speed. Sedges shivered in the shallows. Spanish moss hung everywhere, scraping the boat without sound, ghostly ghastly stuff, wet, gray, hanging in lugubrious hanks.

Could this be the mighty Mississippi? Even when sunlight claimed the middle of the stream for itself, the sullen shore never retreated far. They might have been steaming up some obscure back-country creek. There was no sign of life. No smoke stood up. Not even a dragonfly glittered in suspension above the water. Nothing splashed save the *Tuscaloosa's* paddles, which did so hesitantly, as though afraid. Yet there must be living things somewhere in that wilderness. There must be many such, waiting in silence for the *Tuscaloosa* to pass.

"How can you tell whether it's an alligator or a log?" somebody near Dave and Adoree asked.

"You watch it for a long, long time, maybe half an hour," his companion answered, "and then if it moves it's probably a log."

Now the paddles stilled, and the water that dripped from them slowed . . . slowed. . . . The engines shut off.

This might have been a small sludgy pond in the heart of some swamp. No bird sang, no fish jumped. The air, heavy with a stink of decaying vegetation, pressed in upon them; and though it was hot, they shivered.

An officer touched David's shoulder.

"Captain would like to see you in his cabin."

Dave nodded. Clearly he had been expecting this. He lifted his beaver to Adoree and inclined his head a little. It was the nearest she had ever seen him come to a bow. She had lived all her life among men who looked upon bowing as an art, who moved from the waist as though oiled, being able in this way to express deference, mockery, defiance, respect, indifference, contempt, as a Frenchman might express these with a shrug. David Macdonough was not such a man—and for this reason his slight, shy bobbing of the head touched her.

"Good-bye," he murmured.

"Dave, you—you're coming back?"

He did not answer. He walked away and the officer followed him closely. The officer kept his right hand under his coat, as if on the butt of a pistol. Two deck hands joined the march. Each deck hand held a cudgel, and they watched David Macdonough.

21

The setting could not have been better chosen. Captain Wells was a man with a sense of the dramatic. David stood at the stern, where a jollyboat had been swung out into the chocolate-colored water, a hand at the oars, the second mate in the sternsheets. He stood alone. Deck passengers had been shooed back, and sat or squatted on crates of cargo, staring at him. Above, for all the world like the balconies of an opera house, rose the tiered superstructure, the saloon deck, the promenade, the texas, each a gleaming white ornamented with gilding. All the rails were crowded. Wells played to a full house.

"Let's get this over with," David snarled under his breath.

He did not look directly at the crowd; he didn't dare, for fear of seeing Adoree Sanderson.

As though in obedience to a signal, as though John Wells could command *that* too, the sun slipped behind a cloud. It was dim in this outlandish place now, and murky. The shore leered close on either side.

The furnace doors were open. The heat crinkled David's eyebrows, stung his lips. But the blast of the furnace was as nothing to the heat of Captain Well's words.

Captain Wells had an enormous chest and almost no neck at all. Head back, indignation blazing in his eyes, he posed on the deck and pointed a forefinger at Dave. He said:

"I want you to take a look at this man, folks, so's you'll know him if you're ever unlucky enough to see him again. He's leaving. He would never have come aboard in the first place if I'd known he was a card player."

When he paused for breath the silence rushed in from all sides. The only sound then was a faint protesting *squee* of the jollyboat's painter. David did not look up.

"He admit it?" somebody asked. "He had any kind of trial?"

"Varmits like this don't deserve a trial," Wells roared. "But yes, he admitted it. He told me and my mates, just a little while ago."

The first mate behind him, and the second in the jollyboat, bodded head in assent. They were not in on the secret. As for John Wells, he had missed his calling: so good an actor had to believe what he shouted, at least while shouting it.

22

David Macdonough never once looked directly at the high-banked audience, row above row of faces. The eyes poured loathing upon him, like some foul syrup, and the mouths were set hard. Yet some there must have been who knew a touch of pity. One even spoke.

"Ain't seen him in the barroom," the fellow said. "He's been out on deck the whole time, sparking some female."

"What you say may be true, as far as it goes," called Captain Wells. "But let me ask you this, sir: Can the leopard change its spots?"

"Wouldn't know. Never saw a leopard in my life."

Wells might be short, but he seemed huge when he spread his arms. He was magnificent. Besides anathema, he might have been hurling thunderbolts. There was that about him which suggested the Old Testament prophets —Amos, Ezekiel, Jeremiah, Malachi, Habakkuk—those unpleasant men who got things done.

"That was to lull your suspicions, my friend, so that he could pounce with all the greater ferocity when at last he was ready to rend you limb from limb. Be sure of it: He had no more honorable intentions toward that poor misled female than he had toward your pocketbook."

"You don't have to bring *her* in," David growled.

Wells paid no attention. It is doubtful that he heard. Drunk with his own vituperatory eloquence, he bellowed on.

"Let me show you, my friends, what we took from his pockets a little while ago—and then maybe you will see the need for plucking this viper out of our bosom!"

He produced the gamblers' aids and held them high. They made an impressive array. They must have been in the course of accumulation for weeks, even months, aboard the *Tuscaloosa*. No gambler, howsoever dishonest, howsoever maladroit, could possibly have need for so much apparatus. But the crowd did not know this.

There was a claw, for concealment in the sleeve. And a gooseneck. And a long elastic band, also for the sleeve. And two peeking mirrors, very small. And four crimping rings, surely a superfluity. And colored pencils for marking cards. And a tiny sawed-off section of razor for shaving cards' edges right at the table. There were no fewer than six decks of cards, which, Captain Wells announced in a voice of thunder, had been shamelessly doctored.

All of this, piece by piece, card by card, Wells threw over the rail.

23

"I'll have no such vile stuff aboard the *Tuscaloosa!*" he cried. He faced Dave, his arm an accusation all but archangelic. "And I'll have no such trash as *you!* If you ever show your face here again, by God, sir, I'll send you ashore *without* a boat!"

This was the agreed-upon last line, Dave's cue for departure. Dave turned immediately and stepped into the jollyboat. He held his head high, his back stiff. The oarsman and the second mate gazed at him in horror, as though at a poisonous snake. The spectators, behind him now, hooted and jeered. Somebody threw a bottle and it skittered across the deck and splashed into the water. Somebody threw half a loaf of bread.

It was scarcely a hundred feet, but it seemed miles. In the water around the boat, playing cards bobbed, some face-up, others face-down. David sat in the bow of the small boat, which meant that he faced back toward the steamer, but he resolutely kept his gaze fixed on nothing whatsoever.

A few feet from shore, the mate said, "You can wade the rest of the way. I ain't going to get stuck in the mud because of the likes of you. Go on—jump!"

David's face was hot; he felt little oily blobs of sweat roll down it.

He jumped into the water.

The mud, roiled, sent up billows of black bubbles. There came to his nostrils, as he dragged himself through muck, the evil miasma of the swamplands.

He turned. The jollyboat was already being swung inboard. The great paddlewheels had begun to turn, so that water creamed and hissed. The *Tuscaloosa* lay broadside to him now, and all along the rails the passengers and crewmen stood, not saying anything, not jeering now, but staring . . . staring. . . . They were strips of faces, smeared in his eyes. Which one of them was Adoree?

Well, the show was over. The paddlewheels turned faster. The steamer moved, a majestic sight. Suddenly the steam whistle sounded—high, very loud, a shriek of derision.

That whistle still was sounding when the queen of the lower river slid out of sight, as silently and easily as though the jungle had swallowed it. Then the sound ceased. There were no echoes.

CHAPTER 4

HAD the world gone away and left him? He didn't think so. He believed that he was being watched, that at least one pair of hidden eyes here ashore had observed the scene on the boiler deck. He heard no sound save the gurgle of water among the shallows. He saw no sign. But he had the *feeling* that men looked at him. He acted accordingly. He made no move to explore the place in which he found himself. He scarcely looked around. He had been dumped on the east side of the channel; but whether he was on one of the many Satan's Brood islands or on the east bank itself, he neither knew nor cared.

He took off his coat and placed it on a fallen tree. He unbuttoned his waistcoat. Then he lugged off his boots, which were wet and muddy, like the bottoms of his trousers.

The sun had come out again, but it was shady where he sat. He placed the boots in the sun, clucking and shaking his head as he remembered their former state of impeccable polish.

Then he waited.

It was quiet, an early fall midmorning, and warm. Sunlight dappled the water. Now and then a fish leaped. Once a card, turning, turning, touched the shore near his toes. It might have been trying to catch hold. It tumbled, still turning, and was carried inexorably away. It had been the seven of clubs.

Dave shifted his buttocks, resisting the temptation to dart glances up and down the beach. He got a cigar out of his coat, also a box of those newfangled oxy-muriatic matches. He lighted the cigar. It took an effort to turn his head. He put on his beaver, largely for the purpose of shading his eyes. He placed his hands on his knees.

A long time passed. It must have been close to noon when, for no particular reaon, Dave swiveled his eyes to the right and saw a man about fifty feet away.

This man was staring at David. How long he had been there Dave did not know. He was tall, a scarecrow, not so much dressed in linsey-woolsey as having snatches and scraps of that material sticking to him. His jaw hung slack; his shoulders drooped; but his eyes were as bright

25

as those of a ferret, and a long Kentucky rifle graced the crook of his right arm.

David said coldly, "Well?"

The man showed no sign of having heard.

Dave rose and looked around. Though he could see nothing but hummocks of grass, pickerel weed in clumps, cypress, palmetto, Spanish bayonet, and sometimes the wan glint of water in a pool, he was more than ever convinced that men were watching him. Alligator men they'd be, outcasts who were at home in the swamps, their natural habitat, as cunning there as Indians. But nothing stirred.

Dave unbuttoned his waistcoat and put on his coat. He did this very slowly, turning a little. Gamblers, as the unseen men back there too must know, favored small weapons—a three-inch dirk in a sleeve sheath, or, better, one of those tiny snub-nosed single-shot pistols they called derringers—articles that could be concealed and in an emergency quickly produced, no good at any distance beyond a few yards but extremely effective across a card table. The scarecrow and his hidden friends could not possibly fear, now, that Dave Macdonough carried arms.

His boots were still wet but he pulled them on anyway.

He said to the scarecrow, "You're the man sent to bring me in?"

After a time the scarecrow replied. His voice was not a croak, as might have been expected, but high, querulous, something of a whine.

"I ain't sayin' I is and I ain't sayin' I ain't."

Dave nodded.

"In other words, you ain't sayin'." He brushed the lapels of his coat, tugged down the waistcoat. "All right. I'm ready."

Without even a grunt the scarecrow turned and slouched into the shadows of the swamp. He had a curiously awkward gait, all hips, one that would seem to an outsider the worst possible way to walk here, yet he covered the ground easily and fast—and without making any noise. Indeed, Dave had difficulty keeping up with him. The muck was slimy and he slithered and slid in it, now teetering, now windmilling his arms to regain balance, and at all times so concerned with where his feet went that he scarcely had time to notice anything else. He knew that they had struck straight away from the river, but certainly this did not mean that they were high and dry. They skirted many a pond or tarn, gleaming dark, dull, into which hanks of Spanish moss dolefully dipped. Even away from these the ground gave a sickish sigh wherever he stepped on it. The moss brushed his face, seeming to try with fumbling fingers to cling to him, to hold him back. Though it was hot in there, even steamy, this moss seemed chill to the touch.

All around them as they moved, Dave sensed flitting figures. He couldn't have said how; he never really saw one, definitely never heard them; but he was sure that they were there, ahead, behind, on either side, escorting him, watching him, wraiths in the semi-darkness, gray swampland ghosts, as imponderable as a morning mist, but deadly.

Twice David deliberately skidded to a stop and snapped glances this way and that. All was still. His guide the scarecrow either had not seen him do this or didn't care; he kept going, and Dave had some trouble catching up to him.

"I'm getting winded." For he could hardly pull his breath in this close wet oppressive place. "How much farther is it?"

The scarecrow made no answer. He was not a sociable man. Yet, when he disappeared a moment later—just suddenly wasn't there, like the flame of a whuffed-out candle—Dave Macdonough knew something perilously close to panic. He had to bite the inside of his mouth to keep from screaming.

This passed. He swabbed his face with a kerchief. He swallowed hard. He looked ahead and on either side, seeing no sign. The swamp showed the same as elsewhere, the same as it had been half a minute after they quit the riverbank. It might go on this way for miles. Yet it seemed incredible that the scarecrow, a will-o'-the-wisp, should have taken all the trouble to lure him out here only to desert him. He could not even tell the cardinal directions, so little sunlight came down through the creeper-clobbered trees.

He looked back, and though his footsteps in the mire already were filling, he calculated that for another half-hour he would be able to follow his own trail and thus at least return to the river. Meanwhile, the right way to go might be—ahead. Perhaps the scarecrow had vanished only because he had, so to speak, delivered his package.

27

This proved to be the case. Dave had not gone a dozen steps farther, noting as he did so a slight rise in the ground, when he came abruptly upon a large clearing. In the center of the clearing was a hill, and on the hill there stood a house.

It was a small hill, but a large house, three stories surmounted by a square tower.

What was such a mansion doing out here? He thought he knew, this being government land open for homesteading. Some fifteen or sixteen years ago there had been an exuberent if short-lived flurry in rice plantations. The countryside, many contended, was perfect for this purpose. Fortunes would be made. Everybody wanted to be a planter and live in a grand house, and this opportunity might have been sent from heaven. So they said, anyway. More than one speculator started to build, allowing that he'd arrange for the field labor and the paddies later. Most of them had got no farther than that. The panic of '37 and the subsequent depression wiped them out.

This house, then, was less than twenty years old. It looked at least a hundred. No smoke rose from either of its chimneys. There were many windows but no glint of glass in any of them—whether because it had been knocked out or because it never had been put in—so that the windows gazed at David in blank disapproval. The "lawn" was a litter of knee-high weeds, in places scattered with bones or the charred remains of fires. The building lacked paint, and everything about it sagged. Two of the front steps had collapsed. Half the palings of the veranda rail had fallen out—or in. A pile of trash —cigar butts, fish heads, broken bits of lath and plaster, an old moccasin, potato peelings—was in the very middle of the veranda itself. Flies buzzed about this, as indeed flies buzzed everywhere, keeping up the very devil of a buzz. The place was dreary; it was dirty, and it stank. David Macdonough drew a deep, shuddering breath.

Then he canted his beaver at a cocky angle. He walked out into the clearing. He stood with hands on hips.

"What the hell do you want?" a voice asked.

A man had come out through the front doorway— there was no door. He was a shambling giant who stooped as he walked, his long arms hanging loose. His hair and whiskers were the color of a sunset, while such skin of his face as showed was a lighter red and appeared to be peeling. His nose was venous and very fat. His eyes, like a pig's, were sunk deep down into the face, and they were a very dark blue, almost black.

This could have been the man who had cleaned out the *Tuscaloosa* poker players.

He came down to the ground, moving faster than might have been expected, expertly stepping over the two caved-in steps. He spread his feet and fisted his hips as he faced David Macdonough.

"You ain't answered me," he said.

"Why should I? You knew damn well what I wanted when you sent for me. Now fetch me a drink."

"Listen, you—" The man squinted. "Say, who are you?"

David arched his eyebrows. He curled his lips slightly. "Do you mean to tell me there's anybody left in this part of the world that don't know Captain Flambeau when they see him?"

"Captain Flambeau! You mean—you—"

"Stop · drooling," David advised him. And then: "Didn't you hear what I said? *Fetch me that drink!*"

The man swallowed. "Yes, sir," he said.

Red Whiskers whistled, and from the house there came the very hag Dave had expected, save that she was rather more lumpishly garbed. She wore, as far as he could make out, only a potato sack. Her legs and feet were bare, her head too. She carried a brimming tin ladle.

Red Whiskers was a Rhoderick Dhu of sorts, if a disheveled one, for his whistle garrisoned that clearing with the men whose presence Dave Macdonough had sensed. They did not pop up but rose one by one, languid as smoke, or else sidled into sight from behind trees or around a corner of the mansion. David counted eight of them, and they all looked more or less alike, each a ringer for the first one, the scarecrow. All carried guns, too. They regarded, not their leader, but Dave. Obviously, they had overheard.

Mike Fink on the Ohio, John Henry along the levees, and farther north the fabulous Paul Bunyan: these were names to conjure by. But on the lower river generally, among all classes, afloat and ashore, no name was more awesome than that of Captain Anthony Flambeau.

Some claimed Flambeau was French. Some said Spanish. But most men inclined to the belief that no nation could produce a wizard, a nonpareil, a wonderworker,

29

who must have come from some place outside of this, our world. From Cairo to the Crescent they told tales of his derring-do, of the prodigious feats he had performed—feats pugilistic, ballistic, didactic, frenzied. Truly, they told one another at landing places, in the slave quarters, and on long lazy tied-up nights aboard flatboats and keelboats, broadhorns and barges—truly Captain Flambeau was a ringtailed, mahoganyheaded, brassbellied, sparkspitting sensation straight from Calithumpia Hollow, the offspring of a blue hen, likely enough by an alligator. He was that, he sure was. None had actually *seen* him; but then, how many of them had seen the Devil either?

Dave Macdonough, though well set-up and taller than most, did not resemble Hercules. Moreover, Captain Flambeau in many versions was dark, whereas Dave's hair was a sandy brown. But these were petty details. Any man who even had the gall to *call* himself Captain Flambeau was worthy of respect. They would need proof, these gawkers, but for the present they were his. Even Red Whiskers, though angry, was scared.

"Here you are, sir."

David looked with astonishment at the hag. At close quarters, she turned out to be a girl.

A small girl, this, and from her legs, visible to the knee, David assumed that she was tolerably well-formed, neither fat nor all bone. He couldn't really tell, though, for the burlap—not one sack, as he had at first supposed, but several sewn together—pretty well covered her. The girl's head was exquisite, however, and neatly set on a slim but by no means scrawny neck. Her hair was a very dark brown, virtually black, and straight, and she had drawn it back tight to a bun low on her neck, thus bringing out all the better the shape of the head. Suddenly David wanted to put his hands around that head and caress it, fondle it rather, not for the love of the girl but for love of the sheer shapeliness of the thing itself, as Chinese mandarins used to spend hours turning around and around, and passing from hand to hand, their fingering-pieces of jade.

Also, the girl in the sacking had hazel eyes, and a glowing olive skin, and a mouth that seemed as ripe as it was small.

"You better go 'way, mister," she whispered.

He took the ladle. He knew from the fumes, even before he looked into it, that the ladle contained whisky.

"Haven't you any water?" he asked in a very low voice.

She shook her head. She was standing close to him and looking up at him, looking hard. Her tiny lower lip trembled, and she toothed it.

"Water around here's pizen," she whispered. "You get out—please, mister!"

He shrugged. He lifted the ladle and took as long a drink as he could. There must have been half a pint of liquor inside. It seemed cruelly strong, stinging his throat, but he almost finished it.

"Thank you," he said, handing the ladle back. He found it hard to speak, even hard to see anything for a moment. His eyes tingled, his ears were pounding. He shook his head. "What's your name?" he asked amiably, as the beautiful head came back into focus.

"Sarah."

"Sarah, eh? That's an interesting frock you have on, Sarah."

"Made it myself. My own's wore out. Been here four years and it just plumb wore out."

"I see."

"Oh, I could have plenty of others. Silk ones too. Twenty-thirty of them. But I won't wear anything that's been stole."

"Shut up," Red Whiskers said.

She gave him a glance full of pure venom, then looked at David again. She was an animal in a cage, but David saw plenty of fight in her.

"Sarah, I wonder if you'd be good enough to show me the way to the necessary," he said. "That is, if you've got one here?"

"We got one, but it's mostly me uses it. The boys just go anywhere. Come on."

"Thank you, Sarah. May I?"

He offered her his arm. She shot a look at him, all but baring her teeth. But then she saw that his eyes were mild, not mocking. She nodded, not sullenly, nor with a simper either, and took his arm. She had a great deal of grace for so young a girl.

Ceremoniously, while the men stared, they started across the clearing. The redeye still sang in Dave Macdonough's head as he leaned a bit toward his companion. It was noon and furiously hot, the sun knowing no mercy, so that everything shimmered.

The girl walked like a woman, without fluster.

31

"Go away," she whispered urgently. "Soon as you can! Soon as we get around the back of the house!"

"I came here to take command, not to run away."

"He'll kill you! You don't know Jake Lingle!"

"Can't say that I care to, from what I've seen so far. Are you the only female here, Sarah?"

"Yes."

They walked arm-in-arm, gravely, carefully, she with eyes cast down, he staring into the middle distance, almost as if they were a bridal couple pacing the aisle toward the altar. When they spoke they scarcely moved their lips.

"What are you doing here, Sarah?"

"I cook for them. Fish mostly. I was on a flatboat. We'd come from Cincinnati, and my mother and father died on the way, and the rest of 'em didn't know what to do with me, so they just kept me."

"And the boat was—visited?"

"One night. That was four years ago."

"What happened to the others?"

The girl shrugged. "Nobody ever told me. But I can guess. The head man wanted me, which is why I'm here."

Dave swallowed. "You—you don't look old enough, Sarah."

"I'm old enough, all right."

They walked in silence for some time. They reached the disintegrating front steps but turned aside and went around a corner of the mansion. *The size of her!* Dave thought: *Good God, what kind of men are these?* But he said nothing.

Nor did he look back when, from a faint bumble of talk, he gathered that the watchers had drifted together, perhaps in the middle of the clearing. They must be staring after this curious couple, but it wouldn't do to turn.

They halted. Sarah pointed.

"There it is, mister. Why don't you walk right on past it and into the swamp? Where they are, up front there, they couldn't see you."

"No."

"Jake'll kill you, I swear it!"

"I wish you'd stop saying that."

She looked up at him. She tugged at his coat.

"Are you really Captain Flambeau, mister?"

"I'll be back in a few minutes, and then I want to lie down."

"You ain't, really. Captain Flambeau would never've asked for water."

"So make up a bed for me. And I won't want to be disturbed."

"Yes, sir," she said.

He lay for a long time, not sleeping, not even drowsing, but letting his muscles stay slack and wondering about things. If it had not been for Adoree Sanderson, with her yellow hair, and dark green eyes, everything would be different. He'd put himself into tight spots before, and gotten out of them by not caring too much, but Banker Martineau's niece turned everything around.

Was he a wanderer any longer, at heart? He did not know. For the first time since he had left home he found himself thinking about settling down in a certain place, New Orleans. Oh, he had always thought about settling-down *in itself*. Every roamer does. But now he was dreaming dreams . . . and this could be bad.

It was not a time for dreams.

Even after she had ceased to smile at you, Adoree Sanderson still seemed to be smiling. Her smile left a sweetness surrounding her, like an odor, like the glow of a nimbus. Dave had observed it that night in the garden. Indeed, it had dazzled him then, and he hoped he had not looked as flustered as he felt. And then last night. And this morning, the business on the boiler deck.

He sighed. Tarnation, it was no time to be mooning about Adoree! If he came out of this alive she'd learn the truth, and if he didn't she wouldn't, and that was that.

His immediate concern was the man with the red whiskers.

He occupied a high-ceilinged, square, front room on the second floor, the windows of which were more or less covered by tarpaulins, so that sunlight only squeezed through as planes and spears. The room held no other furniture besides the pallet upon which Dave lay. He could hear, intermittently, a bumble of voices outside. He could not distinguish words. The voices didn't sound angry, yet certainly they were not gay. There was a great deal of going to and from the whisky barrel on the porch.

He would have to fight: he was sure of this. He be-

33

lieved he had done the right thing. They might have their doubts out there, but they were afraid. If it should turn out that he really *was* Captain Flambeau . . .

Nevertheless he would have to fight, no matter what happened.

He turned his head. Ceiling, walls, and floor were stippled and crisscrossed with stabs and streaks of light let in through holes in the tarpaulins or around the edges of these. It made the rest of the room seem even dimmer. Over near the door, a blurred figure squatted, motionless.

"Is that you?" he whispered. "Sarah?"

"Yes, mister."

"Won't they be sore if you're not downstairs to cook for them?"

"Reckon they will."

He could not see her well. He thought of her as a child, and she appeared even smaller now, hunkered down as she was. The position shocked him, but he supposed he'd get used to it if he stayed here long. After all, what was wrong with it? It just seemed to him barbarous because he happened to be used to chairs. He supposed that a heap of folks—maybe half the people in the world, or even three-quarters—had never even seen a chair in their lives.

"I don't want to embarrass you, Sarah—"

"What's that mean?"

"— but I would like to get this straight in my mind. You belong to this man Lingle, do you?"

"Aye."

"I mean, you sleep with him?"

"Have to. He makes me. But I won't wear no stole clothes."

It was an ethical point, Dave reflected, that might have amused and even edified her sisters of the outside world.

"Afore him it was Slatesy," the girl said. "Sol Slatesy. Jake killed him, more'n a year ago. Right out front. Choked him to death."

"I see."

The mumble outside had ceased. And now, as if in response to the girl's statement, the thick voice of Lingle roared:

"You ain't Flambeau! Come out here and tell me that!"

It was a summons. It might have sounded small-boyish to some, but among these seasoned scoundrels, the scum of the rivers, it had as clear and as formal a meaning as any properly carried, written challenge. There would be no conferences and no confrontation by representatives. Weapons would not be examined, measured and weighed, nor watches consulted, nor lines drawn; nor would any surgeon open his little black bag and then straighten up, coughing, to await the worst. Nevertheless, and without being fancy, this was a challenge to fight. Its end was the same as that sought among duelists in more exalted circles—death.

"Come out here and tell me that!" Jake Lingle repeated.

Dave Macdonough swung his legs over the side of the pallet. He tightened his boots. He hitched up his galluses—and then little Sarah fairly hit him with all her body.

"Sneak out back," she babbled. "Run out and I'll yell something, make 'em look the other way!"

He shook his head, gently peeling her off. His eyes still smarted from that tremendous swig of whisky, and there was a stone where his stomach should have been. Still, he guessed he looked all right. He didn't tremble. If nobody else had been concerned, and if the back way had been open for him, he might have slipped out. But he'd be a fool to do it now. They could catch him in no time at all. In this swamp, every inch of which they knew, he'd be at their mercy. He would never know where it came from when they cut him down with lead. He would never have heard or seen anything. And they would leave his body to rot out there, knowing full well that the man who had tried to run away was not Captain Flambeau.

"Pray for me, Sarah," he said solemnly. "I may need it."

"Don't go!"

He put her aside and went down the sagging rotting steps and out onto the veranda. In late afternoon, the blaze of light here dazzled him. He stood a moment with feet spread, his thumbs hooked into the top of his trousers, while he blinked.

There was a great deal of silence.

"Somebody thinks I am not Captain Flambeau?" he asked.

"I do," Jake Lingle said.

Jake threw his head back and his whiskers glistened. He stood naked to the waist. In his right fist he held a bowie knife.

35

"Captain Flambeau," he said, "would be ready to fight."

There was no time to temporize. Dave descended the veranda steps and walked straight up to Lingle.

"I have no knife," he pointed out.

He wondered if Jake was the man who had lifted the watches and wallets last week. And he wondered if Jake had recognized him. It didn't seem likely, though. That masked river pirate had moved fast, stooping far over and keeping his face down. And it didn't matter now anyway.

Lingle lifted his knife. The rays of a setting sun crashed against it. Suddenly, and with a grunt of exertion, he hurled it. The thing flew through the air almost the whole length of this clearing, to fall at the foot of a live-oak about a hundred feet away.

"Why don't you use that one then?" Jake Lingle asked.

Dave looked around, moving only his eyes.

Everybody was watching him. There could be no doubt that this had been arranged. Here was the ceremonious delivery of the final challenge. It was up to him. If he got that knife before Red Whiskers he could use it in any way he wished. This was clear. On the other hand, if Red Whiskers got it first . . .

The river pirates leaned forward, tense, expectant.

No holds would be barred. That was the way men fought on the frontier.

Again Dave looked at Jake Lingle, at the small red angry eyes, the crooked smile. He nodded.

"All right," he said. "I will."

He started to run.

CHAPTER 5

HE sprinted. He could hear Lingle beside him, sprinting too.

In this way, chest to chest, they covered about half the distance. Then Lingle thrust out a leg. He was on Dave's right, and he did this very adroitly, without breaking his stride.

Dave swerved. He missed the outstretched foot that would have tripped him, but as he did so his own left foot slipped on something—he couldn't imagine what—and he fell full-length.

He did not put out his hand to break the fall but instead reached with both arms as far as he could. His right hand caught Lingle's left heel. The bare heel was smeared with mud, yet somehow Dave held on. Lingle pitched forward, the length of his body nearer the knife than Dave.

Lingle slipped and flapped like a speared fish, but Dave held on. Dave even reached out with his left hand and got hold of the bottom of Lingle's left trouser-leg. Then Dave began to crawl and wriggle, working his way hand over hand, clinging to whatever he could get of a bucking thrashing limb, for all the world like a sailor shinnying up a rope in a gale.

Jake kicked viciously with his right foot, rammed Dave's face with his right knee, and even while squirming reached down to batter the top of Dave's head with fists that might have been hammers. Still Dave worked higher. He pinned one of Jake's arms to his side. He got his own arms around Jake's waist. He rolled, heaving.

He had attempted too much. Lingle, too big for him, broke away. Lingle even got up, staggering backward. Dave, on his back, humped up on his shoulderblades and lashed out with both feet, hoping to catch the shins. He missed. Lingle, not fully up, sidestepped, lost his balance, and whirled his arms wildly. Nevertheless, before he fell, Lingle swung his right foot flush for Dave Macdonough's belly. Dave saw it coming, and twisted, bringing up his knees, which diverted some but not all of the force of that terrible kick.

Pain crashed through Dave then like lightning from the sky. It seemed to explode in his head, stunning him. He could not hear anything or see anything. He might have screamed. At least he was sobbing as he managed to get to hands and knees and shake his head, waiting for the end. Just at that moment he could not possibly have struggled. He supposed the fight was over.

Nothing happened.

Gasping, his body drenched with sweat, he raised his head and looked around.

Jake Lingle had toppled smack on his bottom. Dazed, his mouth hanging open, at any other time he might have presented a comic figure. He had been given precious seconds in which to spring for the knife, but the wind had been knocked out of him by his fall. During that crucial instant he was as helpless as Dave.

They stared at one another.

It would have been a good time to quit, if either had been willing to quit.

The men hovered around, leaning forward, their eyes on fire. But they were silent, and they didn't interfere.

Dave and Jake rose at once, like puppets manipulated by the same string or wire. Dave would have sprung again for the Bowie knife, only nine or ten feet away now, but Lingle lurched toward him, bellowing, his big arms widespread.

Dave slammed the man's mouth with short punches, first right, then left, and sprang back. Abruptly Jake's mouth and the whole lower part of his face was covered with blood. But he came on in.

Dave hit him with a high overhand right to the nose. He might have broken that nose. There was even more blood. He jumped back again.

"Stand still, ye sonofabitch!"

It went that way for fully half a minute. The pirate charged sluggishly but steadily, his head low, his arms spread wide, feet wide apart too, as if he were wading through water, while David, steadily in retreat, watchful of those muscle-knotty arms which might crush him, made the man's head bob with blow after blow. Jake's face was a pulp. One eye had closed, and it was almost incredible that he could see out of the other. Yet doggedly he advanced. Dave's hands stung from hitting him, but the man kept coming.

Whether Jake tripped and lurched forward in an instinctive effort to regain balance, or whether he found some spare steam, one last little ounce of energy, Dave did not know. What Dave did know, in a sickening splintering instant, was that he had not stepped back fast enough. The arms were around him.

He went over backward, the pirate on top. Dave must have lost consciousness for a moment. When he came to, the pirate had hunched further up on him, and, either blind or all but blind, was fumbling with sweat-greasy hands for David's face.

Dave knew what he was feeling for—the eyes.

Dave's arms were squeezed between their bodies, and he could scarcely move. He rocked his head. Snapping like a rat, he tried to bite Lingle's hands. But those hands persisted. They groped. They slithered across Dave's face, the thumbs fumbling for eyesockets.

Kill me, Dave thought. *Kill me, but don't gouge my eyes out.*

He had never known such pain. Crushed as he was under the weight of Jake, he could scarcely wriggle. Only one hand was free now. He scrabbled desperately but could find nothing save bare thigh: Jake's trousers, skimpy at best, had been all but ripped off his legs.

No—there *was* something else! It was metal! The knife? It could not be. It was smaller, and not sharp. A torn-off suspender buckle! He got it firmly between thumb and firefinger. He pressed it against Jake's bare leg, inside, high.

"I got it, alligator man! Gouge me—*and you'll crow in soprano!*"

Lingle felt the metal. He squealed.

"No—no, don't do that!"

"Take your hand away," Dave said.

The hands fell off. The great arms went slack. It was only for an instant, but an instant was all Dave needed. Dizzy, his head reeling, he sprang to his feet. He threw the suspender buckle down, and when Jake saw how he had been fooled he let out a great roar.

"Never mind the complaints," David gasped. "Stand up and fight."

He charged.

It had been his plan to stay away from Jake until the pirate tired. He forgot this now. He forgot everything except the bewhiskered face before him. He hit, that was all. He stood and slugged.

He did not know when Jake Lingle went down. He found himself staggering around the clearing, half blinded by blood, mumbling, swinging his fists back and forth, looking for his enemy. Finally he stumbled over Jake Lingle, a Jake who lay motionless. It hardly seemed possible.

The bowie knife still lay where Jake had thrown it, not a yard away. Dave kicked it away. He hooked his thumbs into the top of his trousers. He turned slowly, surveying the men one by one.

"Is there anybody else thinks I'm not Captain Flambeau?"

Nobody spoke. Nobody moved.

39

"Then I guess I'll finish my nap," he said. "Please see that I'm not disturbed again."

He walked back into the house.

Sarah was waiting for him.

When Sarah had finished washing him she covered him with a sheet of coarse linen. All his body stung and throbbed. He lay silent, looking toward a ceiling he could no longer see, for the room was dark now.

He heard Sarah go out with the basin. A little later he heard her come back.

She said, "I prayed for you."

"Maybe that did it," he mumbled, but the situation seemed to call for something more.

"You've been mighty kind," he whispered. "Good night."

"Don't say good night *yet*."

She was getting under the sheet with him.

He propped himself on an elbow and stared down at her. She lay on her back, her eyes aglow in the darkness. She seemed not to breathe.

"Don't," she said. "Please don't look at me that way, mister. You scare me."

"But—you mustn't be here!"

"I don't know where else I'd be. You won, didn't you?"

"But you're only a girl!"

Yet it turned out that she was a woman after all. She was every inch a woman.

CHAPTER 6

SOMETIMES the steamboat disappeared entirely. At other times it poked its bows into a cove so small that Dave could not make it out, even with the aid of the glass. Smoke tumbled from its stacks. It was too far away, north of Satan's Brood, for a watcher in the four-square tower to make out the name. It was white, and the finial atop the texas, as well as the metal filigree work between the stacks, were gilded, so that the vessel gleamed in a late sun. The boat moved cautiously yet jerkily, seeming fairly to *dart*, like a great white-and-gold waterbug.

At last it vanished. Dave folded the telescope, sighing. Here was yet another skipper who didn't intend to take any chances going down among the islands at night. It would be dark in half an hour. Already the west bank shadows were stretching across the water.

So Dave sighed as he put down the telescope. He did not know what he was going to do when the first steamboat skipper *did* elect to run through Satan's Brood at night. Certainly the pirates would attack—intoxicated by their easy success with the *Tuscaloosa*, they could hardly be restrained—and he, Dave Macdonough, just as certainly would be expected to lead them. To refuse would be to break the spell. These alligator men followed him not because they liked him, or because they were physically afraid of him, but because of their awe for the name he bore. He was their chief now. He was Captain Flambeau, and he possessed Sarah, the very symbol of leadership here, as his crown is the symbol of a king's suzerainty. But they lacked loyalty. Let them get it into their minds that he was *not* Captain Flambeau and they would turn on him, stab him from behind, batter his skull in. He knew this. He knew that his life in this outlandish place was not worth a snap of the fingers. Yet though he walked with the lightnings playing around his feet, his step, so far at least, had been steady.

Would that step be steady still when the time for a showdown came? He didn't know. But he definitely hadn't wasted his time. In these eight days he had learned a great deal about the Satan's Brood gang. He had previously decided upon an attitude of outward disdain, as befitting the character of the great Flambeau, an attitude that he wore like a coat of mail. But in truth he was twitchy. They were no fools, these swamp rats. They were dirty, ignorant; nor did any of them delight the eye; but each had the ruthlessness, the cunning too, of a jungle beast. They were as untroubled by scruples as by soap. More—they were alert. They watched him sideways, looking down when he turned upon them, but watching him again a moment later, studying him, biding their time, making plans that were crude perhaps but incalculably cruel. They would spring when they were ready.

Leaving out Sarah, his only friend, they numbered eight. Individually, with a single exception, they meant little to David: they were a blur of dirt and rag. He did not even know most of the names. There was Lingle, whose face, which could never have been a thing of beauty, these days was horribly puffed and discolored:

41

no mistaking *him!* There were the long lank lugubrious Mathewson brothers, Eben and Ik, identical twins whom Dave had privately dubbed the Doorknobs. There was above all the slit-eyed slippery Cateau, a dark thing suggesting oil, a venomous man, certainly the most dangerous of the pack. The rest merged, one into the other, even the massive discredited Lingle—but Cateau stood out. Cateau hated Dave. Perhaps he himself had been the real chief of the band, ruling the lout Lingle, manipulating him. Perhaps Cateau had planned to take over the leadership, including the prerogative that was Sarah. Did he still plan to do this? More than all the others, this one watched David Macdonough.

Cateau seldom spoke. He would squat in silence, without moving, for hours, somehow suggesting a baldheaded buzzard. Yet he was always doing something with his hands, usually sharpening his knife. He handled steel and stone like things he loved, things it thrilled him to fondle, turning them over and over, making no sound. And all the time he watched Dave.

"Thinking about home?"

Sarah had come up through the trapdoor, bearing a cup of coffee.

"Yes, but not my own. I haven't got one. I was thinking about somebody else's home." He took the cup. "Thank you, Sarah."

She tried to seem matter-of-fact, but he could tell she was worried. Her voice trembled a little.

"The boys ask if you'll go down to where they are, mister."

"In a little while," David said.

She meant nothing humorous when she referred to these cutthroats as "the boys." It was but a convenient phrase.

Now she hunkered down, watching David while he sipped coffee. It was good coffee. He would have welcomed it anyway, for it helped to take the taste out of his mouth. The diet, out here in Buzzards' Roost (as Dave called the establishment) was limited, consisting largely of fish, whisky and squirrel, but especially fish, and particularly catfish. "The boys" never seemed to mind, nor did Sarah; but Dave found it a bit monotonous.

"They're up to something," she murmured.

"Yes," he agreed absently.

42

He had felt this coming. Just now, however, he was safe, even comparatively comfortable. A rule of the house allowed nobody up here in the fourth-story tower except the chief and his woman. Not that this was any den of luxury! Its ceiling was cobwebs, the floor a carpet of dust. Glassless, frameless windows pierced the walls. A keg of nails, on which David now sat, was the only furniture: there seemed to be more nails than anything else at Buzzards' Roost, excepting gunpowder. Still, no fishheads were strewn about, as elsewhere. You would not here stumble over a snoring stinking alligator man. The miasma from the swamp itself seldom reached so high. After all, David reflected, everything is relative: in a matter of speaking, this, the highest part of the Roost, constituted its heaven. Besides, the view could fascinate.

From this tower you saw the river. Indeed, you could see for many miles north and south of Satan's Brood, across an undulating sea of oak and cypress—a panorama incongruously peaceful.

David spent a lot of time in this tower. When he first issued the order that it should be reserved for him, and of course for Sarah, his thought had been, his hope rather, that its superior altitude would give him an advantage over the pirates: he reckoned that he would be able to spot any steamboat first, and make plans accordingly. He was wrong, as he soon learned. These ruffians by whom he was surrounded, whose chief and captive he was at one and the same time, seldom looked him straight in the face, but sidled and shuffled, mumbling with averted heads while they didn't miss a thing. They seemed to have eyes that could see through walls. Far from being clever, nevertheless they had a certain animal cunning that sensed peril before peril could strike. Without a word, or so much as a glance at one another, as far as Dave could see, they would pass a bit of information clear around the camp in less than the time it took him to blink his eyes. And they too were scanning the river.

Sarah took his cup and put it on the floor. She sat on his left knee and slid an arm around his neck. She could be as cuddlesome as a kitten. He kissed her.

She said, "Can I look through that thing?"

The telescope, a small brass one, thrilled her. She never tired of it. He opened it for her. She looked north, up the river.

"Do you ever wonder what it's like up that way, the place you came from, Sarah?"

"Sometimes. Not much. Mostly I got too many fish to fry to think about that."

"It's a great big world out there, you know. This is only one little corner of it. Don't you ever wonder what it's like?"

"Well, I wonder what other women are like, yes. And what kind of clothes they wear."

"Poor Sarah! Never even had a chance to be catty! Never had a chance to say disagreeable things behind her fan, and rip somebody's frock apart from the other side of the ballroom! Why, if—"

He stopped, astounded. The girl was weeping. She did not shake with sobs, as one of her more civilized sisters might have done. She tried with some success to hold it in, keeping the glass raised. But her lips trembled, and her eyes abruptly glazed with tears that did not break but hung there, glittering, so that she could not possibly have seen anything through that glass. His hand, held under her left armpit, told him that her heart had all but ceased to beat.

"I'm sorry," he said softly.

He drew her down to him, so that her head rested on his shoulder, while the little brass telescope went clattering to the floor. He held her that way until her trembling stopped.

"I'll make it up for you some day, Sarah," he whispered at last. "You'll have those clothes. I'll bring them to you myself."

She sat up, smoothing her potato sacks. It caught at his throat, that small pathetic gesture. She turned her head away.

"You say that now, mister."

"Don't you believe I mean it?"

"You once leave this place, you won't never dare come back."

"Now—"

"I told you the boys wanted to see you, didn't I?"

"Yes." He frowned. "What do you suppose they want?"

"Probably want to talk about this boat comin' down the river."

He had forgotten the great gold-and-white steamer, which he'd last seen disappear into some cove where he supposed it would spend the night. But there it was

44

again, smoke and sparks standing out bravely from both stacks, fair in the middle of the river, in the light of the setting sun. He needed no glass now. It showed plainly enough. It was so near, in fact, that on the late afternoon air they could hear the screech of steam through its 'scape pipes as it slackened speed preparatory to entering Satan's Brood.

They could not make out the name. As far as David Macdonough was concerned, it might have been *Showdown.*

He knew the moment he saw them that they meant trouble. He loosened the pistols in his pockets.

These pistols, like the bowie knife he now carried, were less for protection than, like Sarah, for the purpose of proclaiming his position. He didn't care for the knife, a heavy clumsy thing. But the Ketland pistols were beauties.

There were shortages at Buzzards' Roost—a notable lack of fine wines, spices, books, scientific instruments, lace, water closet and Shantung silk, to mention only a few—but the place at all times abounded in gunpowder and catfish, as well as the largest collection of firearms David Macdonough had ever seen.

Your frontiersman might be careless in the matter of dress and deportment, and downright slovenly in his speech, but when it came to guns there lived not a fussier person in the world. These weapons at the mouldering mansion on the hill were the fruits of God knew how many raids, how many murders.

Dave had ignored the various muskets and rifles, but he took his pick of the pistols. He pawed over a couple of Forsythes with rosewood stocks, fishtail butts; a huge Lefaucheaux horse pistol, its octagonal Damascus twist barrel exquisitely blued; a couple of Pettingill patents, together with any number of Deringers; a pair of Egg dueling pistols from London; a stunning pair of Richards, with silver name plates, curly walnut stocks, silver ball butts, heavy side strikers. There was even a thick ugly Colt, a queer-looking newly patented repeater, which Dave examined with a morbid interest but which he wouldn't have dared to fire. The Ketlands were a natural choice. True aristocrats, tiny, double-barreled, they were beautifully balanced and very smart with their pearl stocks and chased gold mountings.

45

He always kept the Ketlands loaded. Now, under his coattails, he cocked them.

"What the hell do you want?"

They were evasive, indirect; but in time they came out with it. Did he know there was a steamboat coming down the river?

"Do I look blind?"

What then, they asked bit by bit, was he going to do about it?

"Do? Why, we're going to board it, of course."

Until that instant he had not known what he would say. He heard Sarah, just behind him, give a little gasp.

"But first, you clean up that gunpowder," he cried. "Look at it—all over the floor! Suppose somebody was to light a cigar?"

"But Captain, this boat—"

"God damn it, you heard me! *Clean up that gunpowder!*"

They scurried off, seeking brooms.

It had not been the mere inspiration of the moment, a desire to keep them off balance, that caused Dave Macdonough to storm. A careful man, he had time and again cursed these pirates for the way they handled gunpowder. They were as casual with it as with whisky, in truth treating these two commodities in much the same manner. In the middle of the veranda stood an open hogshead of whisky, from which hung a ladle. They always had at least a few gallons on hand. When it got low somebody would go back to the still—itself loot from a foray—and fetch more. It was much the same with the gunpowder. There must have been tons of it, all stored, or at any rate *kept,* in the ballroom.

That planter who had never got around to planting must have been a man of grandiose ideas. Besides the ballroom, the mansion sported a wine cellar, a large dry clean vault reached by stairs under the main staircase. No doubt the wine cellar never had known wine. It did not even contain-bins. Yet it was a strong place, and several times Dave had thought of transferring the gunpowder there. For the ballroom was peculiarly vulnerable. Several doors led to it, and none was firm, none of the thresholds efficient. The windows, like all the windows at Buzzards' Roost, were innocent of glass, so that breezes could saunter into the ballroom and kick up clouds of gunpowder. A great deal of the stuff lay around loose, just dumped in piles like sawdust.

There was no rule or restriction about the gunpowder. You just walked in and refilled your horn any time you needed to, and if you forgot to close the door when you left—well, all right, nobody was going to raise hell about *that*. Leastways, there hadn't been anybody until Captain Flambeau came along.

The result was that the floor of the main hallway fairly twinkled with black dust much of the time, and the men's feet scuffed it out onto the veranda as well and into other downstairs rooms. They just didn't seem to give a hoot, these fools. Any one of them might have fainted from fright if a black cat crossed his path, yet they did not see anything to get worked up about in the fact that a chance spark could send them double-quick to kingdom come. They thought that this here Captain Flambeau was over-fussy.

Dave felt a tug at his coat, and he turned.

Sarah of the potato sacking didn't remember her own last name; she could not have told a sideboard from a salt cellar, never having seen either; but she did know a heap of other things.

"You're going away," she whispered. "You aim to stay on that boat and go back to the folks you know."

He gaped. It was uncanny. Half a minute earlier he himself had not been sure what he would do next. And almost at the very instant that he decided to skip out somehow—he knew the place well enough, he reasoned, to lead a raiding party back—this child told him to his face what he was thinking.

It was not, strictly, a new thought. Rather it was one of several possibilities he had been considering, though he had only now plumped for it. He had also thought to try to talk the men out of an attack on the first boat to make the run at night, giving as a reason that the steamboat people, put on guard by the *Tuscaloosa* affair, might bait a trap. But these men might be hard to hold, and a counsel of delay would impair his prestige. Most telling of all was the argument that sooner or later he was going to have to face an act of piracy anyway. Why put it off?

Having made up his mind, he weighed two present fears. He could hide aboard the steamer while leading the attack. He knew these vessels, could think of many places of concealment. But could he stay hidden as far

47

as New Orleans? And even if he did, would the pirates, missing him, smell a rat and clear out of their mansion? He did not know. He must contrive somehow to make it appear that he had been killed or captured in the course of the robbery. And after that he must stay out of sight until he got to a place where he could establish his *bona fides*. Found aboard the boat after the others had departed, and identified as one of the pirates, he might be lynched.

Then, too, he hated to think what might happen to Sarah. He looked down at her, smiling a little. He touched her dainty head.

"Don't you worry about me, Sarah."

"I do. You ain't as smart as you sometimes think you are."

"I expect the same could be said for pretty nearly everybody."

"You'll never come back," she said flatly.

"Yes, I will." He took her in his arms, feeling the small sobs that shook her. "I'll come back," he promised.

He did not say how.

But now the rats were ready, and they all went up into the tower—with Dave's permission—for another look at the steamboat.

She was coming, all right. She would enter the Brood. Already lights were appearing at her windows, a wink here, a flash there. Men on the texas deck, tiny figures, were swinging the jollyboats inboard—so narrow was the channel among the islands—and the water of the wake churned turbulent and high as the paddles slowed.

"Get out the masks," said David Macdonough.

CHAPTER 7

THEY could hear the boat for a long time before they saw it. Sometimes it sounded no more than a quarter-mile away, and they could make out the sullen slow thump of the engines, the slap and splash of water as the paddles were halted or reversed. Occasionally they caught even the high "ting" of an engine-room bell. But at other times all sound died as the unseen craft twisted away from them, seeking out a far corridor of the maze. That's how it was in Satan's Brood—tricky even in daytime, even

48

for a small boat. And this was a big boat coming. Only a big boat could have afforded a pilot capable of taking her through the Brood after dark.

David felt sure of this when he heard the fiddles, for only the big boats carried musicians. Oh, there might be some singing among the deck passengers down below, where somebody might even strum a banjo, small boat or large; but these were high-class tunes; in fact, Mozart. The orchestra would be in the dining saloon, and the first-class passengers would be eating now, chattering, laughing . . .

Dave checked masks again and made sure that each man knew what to do. They had three dugouts and the places in each had been assigned. There was no moon. The dugouts were low, and the men, in dun-colored clothing, with no white showing, were to use poles, not paddles. Each dugout had a painter. One would go alongside whichever bow suggested itself. The others would grapple astern, one on each side of the paddles, not too close: they had already ascertained that this was a sternwheeler, this boat coming their way. There was to be no noise. They had prearranged signals, simple ones, not easily forgotten. As in the case of the *Tuscaloosa*, two points only were to be struck—the purser's office and the barroom. The passengers in general were to be left alone.

The music faded, but soon returned, much closer.

The breeze, which had been fitful, uncertain of itself, now died.

The men, their rifles ready, made never a sound. They stayed motionless, without expression, not twitching a muscle. They could go on that way for hours. It was why they were called alligator men.

Suddenly the music ceased. There was a shot, a loud flat sound like that made by two boards clapped together. Then there were more shots. A woman screamed. Men were shouting.

The pirates stared at one another.

"Where is it?" Dave asked.

They could hear the crash of breaking glass, and more screams.

"Be about opposite Hogbelly," Ik Mathewson estimated.

"Just about," his brother Eben agreed.

Dave asked, "That far from here?"

49

"Two-three mile, by channel. Not more'n half a mile cut-across."

The noises ceased, all except the wailing of a woman.

"Could you find the place, at night?"

The Doorknobs stared at him, unable to believe that anybody could ask such a stupid question.

"All right, go there then," he said. "Find out what's happened."

The brothers vanished. It was as though a breeze had puffed out two wavering columns of smoke. They didn't *go*. They simply *ceased to be*.

In less than half an hour they came back. Laconically they told the tale.

Another gang had attacked the steamboat.

"Must be them men camped on Hogbelly Island," Cateau said. "Been there two days. Five-six of them."

"You didn't tell me about them," Dave said.

"You didn't ask."

"They had two boats," Ik Mathewson said. "Guess they stole a heap. They was throwing bags into their boats."

"Why—why, that's *piracy!*"

"Reckon you could call it that."

The story of what had happened to the *Tuscaloosa* had spread. Others were moving in on Satan's Brood, where the pickings were so good.

"We're going to do something right now," David Macdonough announced.

"Join 'em?"

"No. Eliminate them."

It was too long a word for his hearers, but they read in his face what he meant. They nodded, impassive. They loosened their bowie knives, looked to the priming of their guns.

The steamboat came around the bend, moving slowly, like a great wounded animal. It was a blaze of light. Saloon windows sprayed fans of yellow across the water. Torches bobbed on the boiler deck, the rear of which was lit too by a rage-red glare from the furnaces. Men with storm lanterns leaned over the rail, seeming to search for something in the water below. Most of the men had guns. A few carried cudgels.

The steamboat passed within a few yards of the Buzzards' Roost men. They could see the passengers and hands asking one another questions, the officers trying

50

to restore order, a doctor with his bag open, bandages in his hands. They could see the woman who wailed. She knelt amid a litter of broken glass, bending over the body of a boy whose face was gummy with blood.

"Kid got in their way, I guess," Jake Lingle offered.

The boat toiled past. They read her name, brave in gilt letters on white: *Queen of the West*. Then, laboriously, she rounded another bend, her paddles clacking, and was gone.

They could still hear that woman.

After a while David said, "How long would it take to get up to the house and then get from there to Hogbelly Island?"

"With you? Maybe an hour."

"Good. That'd give them time to start celebrating."

"But what do we want to go up to the house for? We got everything we need right here."

"No, we haven't," Dave said.

"What else do we want?"

"Rope," Dave said.

It took them in fact exactly seventy minutes to reach Hogbelly Island and surround the camp.

They saw the light of a fire shining through the trees. They heard the hurrah and the song.

It would seem that the newcomers to Satan's Brood took it for granted that they had the place to themselves, that the men who raided the *Tuscaloosa* had cleared out of this part of the country long since. Either that or they were drunk, or fools, or both. At any rate, they were whooping it up.

David hated what he was about to do. It set all his nerve-ends to tingling and made the pit of his stomach feel as though a heavy stone pressed him there.

He was about to order the killing of five men in cold blood.

It amounted to that. Those five roistering robbers over there, whose shadows swooped and swung as they waved their arms in argument or stamped back and forth, who drank from their bottles, lifting pieces of loot to catch the light of the fire—they would be sitting ducks for the marksmen of Buzzards' Roost. Surrounded, and unaware of this fact, they would never know what happened.

On three sides of them, the swamp hid Dave Macdonough's carefully placed men, and the river formed

51

the fourth side. Two boats floated there, but the *Queen* pirates would not get a chance to reach those boats. They would be cut down to the last man.

It wouldn't be a fight. It would be murder. Mass murder.

The plan was to pick them off from the darkness while they were silhouetted against the light of their own campfire—to start firing at a prearranged signal, giving the men no warning. This plan had been Cateau's, not Dave's. Dave would have attacked openly. But during whispered conferences as they went along, it became clear to Dave that every one of the boys subscribed to the Cateau idea, which indeed was the only natural one for them. Why expose yourself when you can shoot from cover? Why meet a man head-on when you have a chance to attack him in the rear? Captain Flambeau must be mad, even to think of such a thing.

Back at the house he could have scowled the dissenters down. Here in the swamp he was out of his own medium and plumb in the middle of theirs—and his leadership, which meant his life, was at stake.

He had agreed to give the signal.

Now, while he gave his men a chance to get to their places, he told himself, in agony, that he couldn't go through with it.

He knew that he ought to look upon it not as a moral matter but as a business move. These men were competitors; they must be wiped out. He himself had said so, hadn't he? Would *they* have been so chivalrous as to give the Buzzards' Roost gang any chance at all, if the situation were reversed? Had *they* showed any mercy to that boy aboard the *Queen of the West?*

No use. He couldn't do it. Common sense was all very well; but, Yankee though he was, he had a nature rooted in something more solid—and less easily described—than common sense.

He made his decision. He would walk into the middle of that camp over there. He would call upon them to reach for their guns, and as he did so he would draw his own.

He put his hands on the butts of the Ketlands. He started forward.

There was a sound on his left. He turned, his breath caught up.

It had been the agreement that Dave himself would

remain back of this particular curtain of Spanish moss opposite the river bank, in about the middle of the curved line of riflemen. For one thing, the center was the leader's place. For another, Dave Macdonough was an elephant in the underbrush while the others were cats. The less he moved about, the better.

Jake Lingle should have been immediately to Dave's left, at a distance of thirty-five or forty feet. Yet Lingle was not one to make a noise while stalking his prey. Moreover, the sound had seemed to come from much nearer, perhaps only ten or twelve feet away.

Dave took a step in that direction.

In the fitful firelight, broken by moss and leaves, shattered into thousands of small shimmering squares and triangles, it was difficult to be sure of anything. But Dave believed he saw a man kneeling there, a very large man.

"Is that you, Jake?" he whispered.

The answer was a flash of flame, an explosion, a cloud of acrid smoke. Something tapped David on the top of his left shoulder, stinging him about as much as a bee.

He roared with rage, forgetting all plans. He even forgot the Ketlands, taking his hands off them as he ran toward the man who had fired. He wanted to get bare hands on that man before he had a chance to reload.

He assumed that Lingle had slipped into this position in order to kill his chief from ambush—thus jeopardizing the lives of all his companions by settling, as a sneak would, a private grudge against the man who had whipped him.

But it was not Lingle. This one was as large as Lingle but much smoother—a man in a pearl-gray beaver, a bottle-green coat. In the flash Dave caught of it, his was a face of almost incredible cruelty. There was a stiff black mustache. There were stiff black eyebrows that met over the nose, making a straight line. The skin was light, seeming even lighter in contrast to the darkness of the hair. The man was glaring at David, and his eyes were the eyes of a snake.

This much Dave saw as he ran. He also saw that the man, while rising from one knee, had dropped a pistol from the muzzle of which smoke languidly curled. At the same time he was reaching under his coat for something else.

He stepped aside to avoid Dave's first wild swinging blow, but he didn't escape the second. It caught him on the point of the chin and he went backward. He was still tugging at something under his coat as he fell.

Dave sprang toward him, meaning to kick his arm. But Dave's foot struck something solid, probably a root and he fell full-length, his knees and the heels of his hands slithering through slime.

There was another explosion, another flash of orange light, and once again smoke enveloped him. Through it he saw the man with the meeting brows get to his feet. Another smoking pistol was in his hand, and for the second time he had missed David, whose fall had saved his life.

Then the big man vanished.

Dave made no move to follow him. It would be senseless, there in that jungle. What's more, the first shot had of course opened the battle, and the camp behind him now was pandemonium.

He turned and ran back that way. A man sprang toward him, raising a rifle as he did so. He pointed the rifle, and Dave fired both Ketlands. The range was point-blank. The man fell backward as though hit in the chest with a club.

Another came up behind Dave, screaming, brandishing a bowie knife as he bounded along.

Dave drew his own knife and crouched to meet him.

Two shots rang out. The man pitched forward, striking the soft earth with a dull wet sound right at Dave's feet, the knife falling from his lifeless hand.

The battle was over.

Dave went to the clearing, to take charge.

"Who in hell tripped the trap?" Cateau demanded. He wiped his blood-covered knife on the seat of his pants, and lovingly sheathed it. "Couple of 'em damn' near got away."

"One·did get away," Dave said.

He led them to the place where he had met the beetle-browed one, and they learned then that what Dave had tripped over was a carpetbag filled with watches and rings and brooches. The man with the eyes of a snake must have been engaged in giving his fellow thieves the slip—with the cream of the booty. There were other trinkets in the bags at the camp, but the careptbag here held by far the best.

The other thieves would never know of the treachery. The light from the campfire gleamed and flickered now over the five bodies of those who hadn't started to run fast enough.

Only three of Dave's men had been hurt, none seriously.

Bemused then by whisky and watch chains, and very pleased with themselves, the pirates would have left this camp as it was, a shambles. David had other ideas. Now again he drove them, cursing them. Every boat on the river, whether going up or down, had to pass within a few yards of this bank, so narrow was the channel here. Dave planned an exhibit. The outside world should be notified, and in an unforgettable manner, that steps had been taken to stamp out piracy at Satan's Brood—no matter by whom.

There was not enough driftwood to build a gallows, so Dave had "the boys" select tree branches that were more or less in a line with the shore. Each body was suspended from a separate limb.

It was a dirty business, but it had to be done.

Not until the job was finished did Dave give permission to return to Buzzards' Roost.

His head ached, his eyes throbbed. He was afraid he might have to vomit. All the same, he held himself erect, aloof, the great Captain Flambeau, scorning to chat with the others.

In his own room on the second floor, it was different. He refused offers of food and drink. He was trembling now, showing it. He actually permitted Sarah to undress him, at least in part, and for a long while she rubbed his back with vinegar. Her hands were soothing. Later, when she had slipped in beside him, she lay still, letting him hold her tight, not cuddling, not squirming, just lying there. Sarah seemed to understand.

"You don't have to say anything, mister," she whispered. "You just go to sleep."

"Thank God for you," David said.

"Sleep, sleep," she whispered. "Sleep, mister, that's all."

In a rat-gray dawn he woke, and stretched, and missed her. Doubtless she had gone down to the kitchen to get him some breakfast. Still tired, he prepared to go to sleep again. Then he heard sounds in the hallway. He jumped out of bed.

55

In the hall, at the head of the stairs, he came upon an extraordinary sight.

Cateau, who a moment before had squealed like a stuck pig—one of the sounds David heard—now stood shaking with rage, blinking his eyes, while hot coffee rolled down his face and dripped off his chin.

Sarah faced him, spitting furiously. Her hands were full. In one she held a cup, empty now; in the other, a plate of corncakes. Had she dropped either, to slap Cateau's face when he blocked her passage, it might have broken. Crockery was at a premium out here. Sarah had responded to his proposal in a way just as fast and perhaps even more effective: she'd dashed the coffee into his face.

It stung.

Cateau said, "Why, you dirty little—" and went for his knife.

Dave reached him, grabbed his shoulder, spun him around. Fear flared in Cateau's eyes. In that split second when he first faced David he thought he was about to be killed. He was standing at the very head of the stairs, and Dave could easily have knocked him down them, cracking his skull. Certainly Cateau expected him to.

But David only held on to the shoulder.

"Put that knife back," he said quietly.

Cateau breathed again. The fear ebbed out of his eyes, leaving room for hate. But he put away the knife.

"Sarah," Dave said, "is not to be molested or delayed when she's bringing me coffee—*or at any other time.* Is that clear?"

Cateau swallowed, nodded, cast his eyes down.

"All right," Dave said. "Get out. I don't want you hanging around my door."

Sarah tossed him a white-toothed grin. She was proud of him. She started back down the stairs.

"I'll get some more coffee," she said.

Cateau had not moved.

"Well?" David said.

"I come up here to tell you the boys want to talk to you about all this jewelry we got now."

Dave nodded.

"All right. I want to talk to them about it too, as far as that goes. After breakfast."

"But they want—"

56

"I said *after breakfast,* didn't I? Now get the hell out of here!"

He questioned Sarah about it while he ate. She was not flustered. She'd been used to such advances all her life. Cateau, she conceded, had been more than customarily persistent of late, but this didn't worry her.

"I can handle him," she said. "The only thing is, if he turns them *all* loose on me, then it would be bad."

"I can see that."

"But he won't—as long as you're here. He's scared of you."

Dave Macdonough was thoughtful when at last he went downstairs to meet the boys.

This was a conference long overdue.

The mansion atop the hill was heaped high with swag that rotted or rusted many miles from any place where it could be put to use. There were bales of silk and bolts of calico. There was a great deal of rope, and, as mentioned, gunpowder. There were the guns. Unexpectedly there were many musical instruments: a French horn, two flutes, five banjos, no fewer than twelve fiddles, a double bass, even a harp. Two rooms were packed with kegs of nails, presumably floated all the way from Pittsburgh for sale along the line or at New Orleans, where metal objects were always in demand. And there were also hinges and clasps and padlocks, hammerheads, axe and hatchet heads, flatirons, sadirons, andirons, haywire, knife blades. . . .

The treasure itself was a mixed bag.

Dave might have supposed that the pirates would thrill at the sight of the bijouterie they'd netted. It was not so. They must have known that these articles had value, but to them it was like owning a complicated machine which they couldn't operate, or even start. All they could do was look at the things in wonderment, baffled.

The pre-*Tuscaloosa* gleanings were pitiful, wrenched doubtless from the poorest class of traveler. There were six or seven silver watches, two of them with chains; a cracked miniature; a silver brooch; eight wedding rings, one set with a small diamond; a couple of cheap bracelets; a lavaliere of little worth; a crucifix on a thin gold chain.

Captain Wells' luxury steamer had yielded a fancier haul. Everybody in the barroom the night of that momentous poker game, even the bartender—everybody,

57

that is, excepting Dave Macdonough—had been robbed of some sort of jewelry. Dave recognized Judge Ryerson's watch, a gift from his daughter, the one he had said he would give a thousand dollars to get back. He recognized a couple of costly rings too, torn from the judge's old thin aristocratic fingers. He recognized many another piece. These were good gauds, not gimcrackery.

The slaughter at Hogbelly had paid off even more handsomely. The intruders, it would seem, had gone right in among the first-class passengers caught at dinner, and without troubling to turn out pockets had snatched and torn away right and left, promiscuously dumping everything into bags—rings, bracelets, bangles, barpins.

"That stuff," David announced, "is worth a great deal."

"Not to us it ain't."

"Not out here, no." He looked around. This was the time to strike, while the iron was hot. "But you're not going to stay out here long."

"Huh?"

"You fools, you had to wait weeks after the *Tuscaloosa* for another boat to try the run. How long do you reckon you'll have to wait after what happened last night? Months!"

"Well, we been here four years now," Jake Lingle pointed out. "We got lots of time."

"And what if a posse appears?"

Jake waved his hand. "Then we go back there."

He meant that they would disappear into the swamp, to live there until the raiders had departed. They were perfectly prepared to do this, as Dave knew. He nodded grimly.

"And leave this, I suppose?" He pointed to the pile of jewelry. In the nature of things, he knew, to move fast in the swamp meant to travel light. "Handy to carry, isn't it?"

They were dashed. This had not occurred to them.

"But with *money*—bank bills, not gold—you could flit as you liked. Yes, and wherever you fetched up you'd be rich men."

"We—we got money," Ik Mathewson said.

"*That* hatful?" Dave patted the pile of jewelry. "This is worth ten times that, if you sell it in New Orleans."

"And who's going to sell it in New Orleans?"

.He was prepared for this. "Why," he said, "I am."

They stood staring at him, not directly but obliquely, through shaggy eyebrows. They had to ponder this.

"You know somebody'll buy that stuff?" Ik asked.

"Of course I do."

He was Captain Flambeau. He wasn't consulting them or asking their advice. He was telling them.

After a while Eben Mathewson asked, "How would you get to New Orleans?"

"You could slip me aboard the next downboat while it's passing Hogbelly. They always go quarter-speed there, and everybody'll be looking at the bank—looking at what we left there last night. Once I get aboard I'll find an empty stateroom somehow, and then I'll just sit tight."

"And what if you get caught, with all that stuff?"

Dave shrugged. "Then I guess I'd be hanged. There's a lot of hard feeling against pirates along the lower river these days. It isn't likely I'd be turned over to the law."

"And where would that leave us?"

"Why, right where you were when I first found you. On the other hand," David went on, "if I make it I'll come back with plenty of money for all of us."

There was a considerable silence while they thought about it. Several shook their heads. Others drifted out to the veranda for a dipperful of whisky, and returned wiping their mouths.

At last came the vital question, the one they were all asking in their minds—even Sarah, who stood behind Dave now. It was Jake Lingle who voiced it.

"How do we know you *will* come back?"

Dave contrived to look outraged. He clenched his fists, Jake went pale. But in a moment Dave shrugged, turning away.

"I'll come back all right," he growled.

It was his turn to go pale when he caught sight of Cateau, that poisonous little man with the letterslot mouth, who was watching Sarah now. Cateau had more imagination than all the rest of them put together, and not a scrap of conscience.

"He'll come back," Cateau whispered, never taking his eyes off Sarah, while he sharpened his knife. He ran the tip of a bright pink tongue across his lower lip. "He knows what'll happen if he don't. Sure, he'll come back."

He went on sharpening his knife, and looking at Sarah.

CHAPTER 8

AROUND David and Lingle, as they crouched in a dugout, the stink of Satan's Brood was like fog. The mud in the shallows, decayed weeds, the stagnant scummy swamp water—they all stank, but the most penetrating odor came from the bodies that dangled on the shore of Hogbelly Island. Buzzards had worked assiduously for three days, but the bones, the clothes, and the smell remained.

Jake and David could not see the bodies because of a steamboat.

Three steamers had gone upriver in these past two days, but this was the first to come down. The passengers and hands would have heard of the grisly sight on Hogbelly. They'd be lining the starboard rail, morbidly fascinated.

The reach was not a broad one as the open river went, but it seemed broad here in the Brood. Dave and Jake waited among the sedges on the opposite side from Hogbelly, near the lower end of the reach. They were screened by Spanish moss that hung from trees.

"Remember, now," Jake whispered, "what Cateau said we'd do."

"I am not likely to forget," Dave said coldly.

Nor was he. The oily little man with the slit eyes had gone into detail, and his plans were more than merely lecherous.

Dave had kissed Sarah tenderly.

"You take care of yourself now," she had pleaded. "You stay there, where you'll be safe."

"I'm going to get you out into the world, somehow," he told her. "It isn't fair. You've never had a chance."

"Never you mind about me." She found a grin, though it came hard. "I can take care of myself. I'll give 'em what-for, they get fresh with me." And, as she nestled: "Just be careful, mister. Be awful careful."

In David's ears still was Cateau's voice setting forth what would be done to this girl if her protector didn't reappear. Dave swallowed, and his eyes felt hot.

A shot sounded, a hollow boom. Dave parted the moss and peered out. The steamboat was close now and he could read the name: *Maid Marian.* There was nobody in sight on this side, the larboard side. That was what they had hoped for. They had a diversion ready. The other boys were hidden in the forest just below Hog-belly, on that same side of the channel, prepared to beat pans, yell bloody murder, perhaps even shoot off a few guns, should this be needed to draw attention. It wasn't.

Sternward of the texas a white blob of smoke tumbled. Somebody had fired a shotgun at the busy buzzards, not in the hope of killing any at that distance, or even hurt-ing them, but in order to drive them away from their feast for a moment. He had succeeded. The birds rose in lumbering circles, not uttering any cries, but stretching their necks and rustling their dry wings. They did not fly far. They soon settled, ready to return to the meal the moment the coast was clear. One landed on a half-sub-merged log or sawyer in the water not ten feet from where David was, and it fussily huffed up its rusty-brown feathers like an old woman resetting a shawl, and then drew in its bald head and regarded Dave with small red obscene eyes. Its beak slobbered with blood.

Dave looked again at the steamboat. He dug in with his paddle.

"*Now!*"

Jake Lingle, too, dug in with a paddle.

They were large men, and the carpetbag between Dave's knees was extremely heavy, but the dugout itself was a small light one, and they made good speed, bend-ing low to the task.

They had gauged the distance well. The steamboat, about to leave the reach and enter one of the narrowest parts of the channel, was barely moving. They came alongside without a bump just astern of the larboard paddlebox, where the water was not turbulent, as or-dinarily it would have been, for the paddles barely turned. The deck was low, back near the landing planks. Lingle held the boats together while Dave Macdonough easily scrambled aboard the *Marian*. Then Jake stood up in the dugout, and with a tremendous effort hoisted the carpetbag onto the deck. After that he pushed the dugout off, sat in it, and produced a pole and line—becoming, in a flash, just one more frowzy frontiersman in search of fish.

Dave stood on the deck and looked around. He had never before been aboard *Maid Marian*, but a glance showed him that her rear was built much the same. as that of any other large river steamer. He had expected this. He would know where to go, where to seek a stairway to the upper decks. What interested him more was his reception, if any. Half a hundred persons might have seen him as he climbed aboard, had any of them turned. But men and women, above and below, passengers and crewmen alike, had had eyes only for the gruesome sight on the shore.

Hastily Dave picked up the carpetbag. It was the same bag he had tripped over when the blackbrowed stranger shot at him, and now, three days later, it weighed even more. Lugging the bag, he made for an after ladder.

Up two decks, he found himself in a corridor, one side of which was a blank wall, while the other side consisted of cabin doors. Each door bore the name of a state— New Jersey, Delaware, Maine, etc.—which is why they were called staterooms. A few doors had keys in the lock; most stood blank. All were closed.

There was nobody in sight.

The doors with keys in them, he assumed, would lead to empty staterooms. It was the customary practice.

He went to the nearest of these—it happened to be Pennsylvania—unlocked it, and let himself in. He locked the door behind him. He sat down, exhaling in relief.

So far, so good.

Pennsylvania, though small, was scrupulously clean. There were two berths, upper and lower, both made up. There was a let-down washstand, a small wardrobe, a chair, a cane mat, a slopjar. At the far end, a window opened upon the promenade deck. It was covered by a jalousie, or sun shutter.

But this small world was encapsuled in a larger, noisier one. The engine, slow, stolid, reluctant, shook the whole boat. There were voices in the corridor, as, Hogbelly being out of sight, the passengers returned from the rail, bringing voices and the sound of footsteps through the window. Somebody tried the door. Dave stiffened, his hands on the pistols under his coat. Whoever it was, laughed and went away . . . a mistake. Soon somebody entered the cabin on the left, Indiana, and later somebody entered Georgia, on the other side. There were two persons in Georgia, and they moved about a good bit, frequently bumping the thin wall. Dave assumed that they were husband and wife, for they quarreled in a

tired, dogged way, without pause. There were footsteps
above him too, while from below rose the clean "cling!"
of engine room bells and the mumble and shuffle of deck
passengers.

On the river, David Macdonough had few acquaintances. He ate alone whenever he could. The men he did
know were mostly those with whom he played cards. But
now he was a marked man. Several hundred pairs of eyes
had been fixed on him when he was thrown off the
Tuscaloosa. Those folks would remember him, and raise
an alarm the instant they saw him on a steamboat. Only
two weeks, or a little more, had passed since the *Tuscaloosa* had made the upriver trip. Some of these passengers aboard the *Maid Marian* might well have been
aboard the *Tuscaloosa* then. Or they might have been
casual acquaintances who had heard what happened to
him. In either case he could not afford any investigation.
The contents of the carpetbag he carried spelled murder.

He put the bag on the upper bunk, and took off coat
and boots. He had no need to wash and shave.

Suddenly he wheeled, facing the window.

It was as definite a feeling, and gave him as much of a
start, as though somebody had spoken or had reached
out to touch his shoulder.

There was nobody at the window. *Had* there been?
People were passing out there on the promenade, their
shadows sliding slowly across the slotted bars of sunlight.

Dave shook his head, impatient with himself. He was
getting nervous. He went to the window and found that
it was not only shut but stuck. He would not be able
to get it open without making a great deal of noise,
probably using a tool, and this he wouldn't risk.

True, the slats of the sun shutter were all but horizontal, so that a person on deck, squinting, could have
seen most of the inside of the cabin. Dave adjusted these
so that they pointed up, permitting a view of nothing
more than the ceiling. He should have done this the first
thing after entering Pennsylvania.

He unstrapped the carpetbag and rearranged the articles on top—a pathetic attempt to make the contents
seem, at a glance, ordinary. Packed above the brooches
and barpins, the necklaces and watches, bracelets and
bangles, was burlap sacking. This served to some extent
to keep the pieces of jewelry from clanking and clicking

63

together. It also served to cover them in such a way that they would not be instantly visible to anybody who opened the bag. Laid out on the burlap, in sight, were the few personal things Dave Macdonough possessed—an extra handkerchief, toothbrush, razor and shaving soap, a small towel. These did not convince. He wriggled a hand underneath them and touched the telltale trinkets.

Most of the articles in that bag could easily be identified as loot from the *Queen of the West*, taken in the course of a raid in which a boy had been killed. It would go hard on the man who was found with them in his possession.

There was a knock on the door.

Dave closed the bag but made no other move for half a minute, hoping that here again was a mistake.

The knock was repeated.

Pistol in hand, he went to the door. He put his ear against it. He could hear somebody breathing out there in the corridor.

"Who is it?" he called.

Maid Marian by now had extricated herself from the maze called Satan's Brood and was booming down open river all smeared with sunset. From time to time she tooted her whistle, either in signal to the men at certain landings she wasn't touching or else out of sheer exuberance, like a cock in a barnyard. Under full steam the boat shook violently. The voices outside were more animated as the sun dipped low. Every now and then a playful current of air sent a swirl of soot from the stacks down under the hurricane deck and onto the promenade, and then Dave could hear women squeal in dismay, while men, tut-tutting, drawing handkerchiefs, gallantly rushed to their assistance.

There was another knock.

A voice came through the keyhole—a low voice.

"Open up, if you know what's good for you, Macdonough."

Dave drew a deep breath. He opened the door.

This man was about forty. He had ice-blue eyes, a mouth made of steel, hair gray at the temples. His neckpiece was dark blue, his coat black. On his head he wore a stovepipe. There was a large plain gold chain looped across his dark blue silk vest. There was an enormous table-cut diamond in a ring on one of his fingers. He was not a tall man, though the stovepipe made him s'eem so, but he was broad in the shoulders.

Now he smiled. It was not a pleasant smile.

"May I come in?"

"No," David said.

But the man already had slipped a foot into the doorway. Dave could not risk the sound of a scuffle. The stranger stepped aside.

"After all, Macdonough, if I was to raise a fuss we'd *both* be booted off at the next landing, eh? So why do that?"

He sat in a chair. He jerked his head up, to indicate the window.

"Got a glimpse of you. Flummoxed me. Can't imagine when you came aboard. I watch 'em mighty careful, I can tell you."

"What do you want?" David asked.

"I want to talk to you." The man lighted a long cigar with hands that were marvelously steady—clean hands, blue-veined, strong. "And you better listen sharp, Macdonough. Your life depends on it."

CHAPTER 9

SENATOR John T. Alsop was not a senator. Titles were taken for granted in this part of the world. If you had any pretensions to gentility you would no more go around without a handle before your name than you would go around without your pants on. Indeed, you wouldn't be permitted to. They would *give* you a rank, come willy come nilly. Servants in particular found it convenient to bestow titles. It was believed to flatter the person waited upon. "Boss" or "sir" might be used in addressing just anybody—a man, that is, who didn't look like a tip—but something more distinctive should be used for quality folks. "Captain" could be applied to a young man, unless he was mighty stern of mien, in which case he could be promoted to "major." Any man over forty who could stand upright was of course a colonel, unless, being of especially distinguished appearance, he was a judge, a senator, or a governor.

Those who did not have a legitimate title, or didn't have one awarded them, usually did as John T. Alsop had done—they adopted one. In fact, they always adopted one, if, like Alsop, they needed it for business purposes.

David's visitor, Senator Alsop, was one of the most notorious gamblers on the lower Mississippi, a crack pistol shot, a master of rough-and-tumble, venomous as a rattlesnake, clever as a fox. As to his courage, it was a measure of this that he ventured to book aboard a big steamboat. True, he wore a disguise. Your gamester ordinarily was clad in flamboyant raiment and hung with all the gewgaws he could afford. The black coat, the somber cravat, most of all the stovepipe, must have made Alsop wince inwardly; but they constituted the best he could do in the way of protective coloration as long as he was rash enough to walk right into the enemy's territory.

"What do you want?" Dave said again.

"You're laying low, I take it, Macdonough? Well, that's sensible. That's what I ought to be doing myself. I started to. But then—well, two suckers came along and just about *insisted* upon being taken. So I've got a game scheduled for tonight."

"I see."

"I'm sure you do. It's my game. I'll set the stakes. I've bought the bartender who'll sell us the cards."

"Cards you've already steamed open and worked on?"

"That's right. Any other time I'd be glad to say 'Sit right in, plenty of room.' After all, that's no more'n professional courtesy."

David said nothing.

"But tonight's different. Too much at stake. I don't want you to come anywhere near that barroom, Macdonough. Understand?"

Dave said slowly, "So that's what you came here to tell me?"

"That's what I came here to tell you."

He rose. He took the cigar out of his mouth and made tiny jabs with it toward Dave's chest. There was not much room, and they stood close together. The walking beam pistons scree-ed and thunked. Bells rang below. The couple in Georgia squabbled on. Somebody walked along the corridor, banging a gong. "First call for dinner!" Aft, somebody plunked a banjo, dolefully singing:

> "Buffalo gals, won't you come out tonight,
> "Won't you come out tonight,
> "Won't you come out tonight?"

"Because if you do, if you so much as set a foot in that barroom," Senator Alsop said, "*I'll kill you.*"

He put the cigar back into his mouth.

"Don't make the mistake of thinking that that's hot air, either, Macdonough. There's ways of making it look like self-defense. And I've got connections."

Dave said, "Get the hell out of here."

"Temper, temper! Why, of course I'll get out. Didn't you hear that gong? I don't know about you, but *I'm* hungry. Good night."

And then he left.

Dave lay for a long while, pondering. In a pocket he fingered a torn-off suspender buckle, the one that had saved his eyes in the fight with Lingle. He hoped he wasn't superstitious; but all the same, he intended to keep this buckle as long as he lived. He hoped too that he was not afraid of being afraid. He had no code to live by. He was alone, as he had been alone, to all intents and purposes, ever since he left home. He could indulge in cowardice and nobody would be the wiser—except himself.

> "*Buffalo gals, won't you come out tonight,*
> "*And dance by the light of the moon?*"

He knew Senator Alsop was desperate. Alsop could not go on playing the lower river boats much longer; he was too well known and the campaign against gamblers was too hot. To go elsewhere required a stake. Here he had a melon ready for the cutting—and then, fortuitously, he'd learned that there was another member of the profession aboard. He had reacted in a way that was perfectly natural to him. What's more, he meant what he said.

Nevertheless, Dave Macdonough, who a few minutes ago had not dreamed of visiting the place, now felt a tug in the direction of the bar.

Dave did not like to be told where he could go and where he couldn't go.

This was the height of folly, and essentially Dave was a hard-headed man. He reminded himself, too, that he had others to think of. Maybe he *wasn't* alone, after all? What about his duty to his employers, the money men? His promise had been to clean out the pirates of Satan's Brood, not merely to come back with a bag full of booty.

67

And there was Adoree. An explanation was due her, as well as an apology. And also there was Sarah. . . .

He rose, his ears ringing, his heart thumping. He would get over this crazy impulse, he told himself.

> *"Won't you come out tonight,*
> *"Won't you come out tonight?"*

Air: that's what he needed. Pennsylvania was stuffy. Senator Alsop's cigar had not been to Dave's taste, certainly not in these confined quarters. He cocked his head, listening. The couple in Georgia had quit their quarrel and gone out. He heard no footsteps in the corridor. Nobody had passed on the promenade for some time. With the boat not filled, he reckoned there would be only one dinner sitting. No doubt everybody was in the dining saloon right this minute. If he was going to get a breath of air—and he thought he'd be sick if he didn't—this was the time for it.

He put on shoes, coat, beaver. He ignored the lamp, though the cabin was dark now.

He opened the door an inch, listened, then stepped out.

He tilted his beaver over his eyes, hunched up his shoulders, thrust hands into pockets, and made for a deck door.

Outside he felt better. It was dark, a quiet night. The river was wide at this point, and *Maid Marian*, fair in the middle of it, was making good time. The shore showed not a pinpoint of light. The stars were popping out, pert, alert.

The air was delicious. He gulped great lungfuls of it.

He'd take one turn around, maybe two, he thought, and then duck back into Pennsylvania before the first of the diners emerged.

A familiar voice said, "Why, *David!*"

He whirled around, and found himself face to face with Adoree Sanderson.

Dave raised his hand to his hat, blocking off his face. "Some mistake, ma'am," he mumbled.

He walked away, taking long strides, all but running. He heard her cry "David!" and start after him. She *was* running.

The sign "Bar" loomed on his left, and he nipped through that door like a rabbit diving into its burrow. He

68

was just in time. The footsteps had almost caught up with him.

No women would be permitted to enter the barroom, even if any were so brazen as to try. He had cut himself off from Adoree as effectively as though he'd slammed a steel door in her face.

Still, she could wait outside. She could blockade him. And soon the poker players would come, including Senator Alsop.

Whatever he did must be done quickly. To linger would be fatal.

He *might* have time to explain to Adoree and warn her to ignore him, before folks began coming up from dinner. More likely he wouldn't. And if he were subsequently arrested, and the damning evidence of the carpetbag found upon him, the fact that he had been seen talking to her might come out, wrecking her reputation.

There was too much to tell her: that was the trouble. Even putting aside his vow of secrecy, given to the money men in New Orleans, he could not, in a few words slipped out of a corner of his mouth, bring her to understand the reason for his concealment. She would naturally demand to know more. She had every right to do so.

And now—what?

He looked around. The room was long and narrow, with one large round table, obviously for cards. Everybody was at dinner. The only person present was the bartender, who put down a sleazy gray towel.

"Good evening, sir."

Now Dave saw with delight that there was a door at the other end, a deck door to boot. This was one of those barrooms that went the whole beam of the boat. Perfect! He started across.

"What'll it be?"

Abreast of him, Dave nodded and smiled.

"Beautiful evening, isn't it?"

He walked right on past and out the other door.

"Sonofabitch," said the bartender, and picked up his towel again.

On the larboard side now, David really did run. Adoree could not half-encircle the boat and cut him off here, in the time he had used to cross the barroom; but he took no chances.

69

Two minutes later he was back in Pennsylvania, with the door locked.

Meeting the girl had been a shock, yet it had not been altogether unexpected. Back in Buzzards' Roost, when he first thought of this manner of returning to report, he had taken into consideration the possibility that Adoree might be aboard the boat he hopped. She was visiting kin near Vicksburg, and a visit like that, for a person of her class, ordinarily would last at least a month. But she had told him aboard the *Tuscaloosa* two weeks ago that because of the serious illness of an aunt in New Orleans she had for a while thought of calling the trip off, and she might yet be obliged to cut it short if bad news came north by another boat. Dave knew now that this must have happened. He had even thought, though fleetingly, of going to the office and asking to see the passenger list, to learn if she was aboard. He'd discarded this idea because he feared that the purser might get to wondering who he was. A purser should know every passenger, at least by name. No, he had better remain right here—with the carpetbag.

That bag! He glowered at it. It was a millstone around his neck, a Damoclean sword suspended above his head, the Old Man of the Sea firmly fastened, an incubus, on his back.

He would gladly have dropped the thing over the rail; but he had no right to do this, since it wasn't his property.

He was getting hungry. He lay in a bunk and tried not to think about it.

Maid Marian was a gay boat. He could hear music, laughter, people passing.

Some time between half past nine and ten o'clock the situation got too much for him. It was a case of nerves, a malady from which Dave seldom suffered. He knew what he *should* do. He should sit tight, not opening the door or lighting his lamp, not even moving around.

What he did do was draw the charges from the pistols and reload these, and then put on his hat and go out.

He would avoid Adoree: of that much he was determined. But he'd be damned if he was going to have a cheap bully like Alsop tell him where he should go and where he shouldn't. This was childish, and he knew it. Nevertheless he headed for the barroom. It was as though he had no choice but was drawn there by magnetic force.

He did make himself pass the place once, going forward for a peek through the windows into the ballroom. It was a bright scene, the men in their black coats and snowy stocks, the women in flounces and furbelows. He listened for a time to the tinkling talk, and wondered, a whit glumly, whether he would ever fit into a life like that. At the same time, he wondered whether he wished to.

Adoree was dancing, with an easy unthinking grace, in the arms of an extremely tall young man.

She belonged in a ballroom. If Dave had some difficulty picturing himself in that sort of company, he would have had even more difficulty picturing Adoree Sanderson anywhere else. When he let himself think of that girl, which was not often, it was not to dream of carrying her off to a far place. That, he knew, just wouldn't do. If he took Adoree he would have to take New Orleans with her, which meant that New Orleans, a choosy city, in turn would have to accept him. And naturally Adoree too would have to take him, in the first place.

He shook his head, out there on the deck. Was he getting a mite silly? Maudlin? He lighted a panetela, and made for the bar.

He saw about twenty customers, and the room was blue with smoke. Few stood at the counter itself. Most of them were watching the game, at which seven played.

The seven, of course, included Senator Alsop.

"Change your mind?" the bartender asked.

"Yes. Give me a flip."

"Whisky?"

"Yes."

Dave had cocked his beaver low over his eyes, but Alsop would recognize him—if he looked. As far as Dave could make out, Alsop had not glanced up. But he wasn't too sure. An operator like that might see around corners.

Dave noted that Alsop did not have a notably tall pile of chips. Any one of three things might account for this, and Dave decided that before he joined the game he would study it for a while and deduce which of the three prevailed.

For he fully intended to play. He knew this was foolhardy; but he was aware as well that the laws of common sense are not the highest laws known to mankind, and that if a man always listened to the voice of reason he would become a gibbering idiot.

71

Alsop might have sold chips to losers just before Dave entered.

Or Alsop might still be playing with undoctored cards, biding his time, waiting for the others to get overconfident or perhaps drunk, for the stakes to be raised. *Then,* when he was ready for the killing, he might throw a fake fit of exasperation and tear up the present deck, or part of it, and on the plea of superstition purchase another deck from the bar, a prepared one. This was a common trick among crooks.

Finally, Alsop might have a capper. It was this possibility, the one which seemed most likely, that gave Dave pause. If somebody was working with the senator, Dave wanted to spot that somebody.

At first the game seemed even. Nobody was moaning-and-groaning much; neither was anybody openly exultant. Nobody's pile was mountainous, nobody's was countable at a glance. The betting was not remarkably high, though it was fast. A cheater liked a fast game.

Dave ruled out the men on either side of the senator. Men playing signals prefer to face one another. Of those farther away, the most probable seemed a large stout sleepy-eyed man, a rather frowsy fellow who answered to the name of Ellis. He sat almost directly opposite the senator. He had the most chips. Whenever he dealt, Alsop won. Whenever Alsop dealt, Ellis won. Each, apologizing, made an excuse to ask the other to repeat his name. From these and a dozen other small signs, Dave concluded that Ellis was the capper, the one to be watched.

The second possibility was not to be ruled out, however. If Alsop did feign impatience and call for a new deck of cards, or if Ellis did, he would be sure to take the top deck of those piled behind the bar. This would be to make it public, plausible.

Dave eyed the pile of boxed cards behind the bar. Six or seven decks, in two stacks, piled very neatly. They all looked sealed; but Dave Macdonough knew how much an expert could do with steam.

He paid for his whisky, then tossed a quarter on the bar.

"I think I'll have a deck of cards. Play myself some solitaire."

"Sure."

The bartender moved between the cards and Dave,

72

keeping his back to Dave. Prepared for this, Dave stepped to one side and caught a glimpse of the reflection of the man's hands in the mirror.

"The *top* deck, please," Dave said.

Aggrieved, and with a guilty flush, the bartender muttered that they were all exactly the same anyway.

"I said the top deck."

He got the one he demanded. He put it into a hip pocket.

"Thought you was going to play solitaire?"

"I've changed my mind. I think I'll play poker instead."

He shouldered his way to the edge of the table, to a place opposite Senator Alsop, and next to the fat Ellis.

"Is this a private fight," he inquired, "or can anybody get in?"

CHAPTER 10

THERE was no explosion. Alsop, like the others, looked up and nodded impersonally. They said, "Sure, sure!" and "Sit down, sir!" They tossed their names at him, and he gave them his as he slipped into the chair on Ellis's right.

Your operator of a rigged game is prone to burst into anecdotes, witticisms, wry remarks about Lady Luck, and the like. He talks a great deal, lightly, distractingly, his purpose being the same as that of the sleight-of-hand performer who with his patter causes the attention of the audience to veer away from the deeds he doesn't want seen. Alsop did not behave this way. He was quiet, even absent of manner. He spoke only to pass or call or raise. He had scarcely glanced at Dave Macdonough. He seemed absorbed in his hand.

David was not deceived. Alsop's ice-blue eyes had been trained to conceal emotion, as those of an actor are trained to show it. Alsop had not forgotten his promise. He was biding his time, waiting for an opening. Dave Macdonough played poker automatically. not with the intensity with which he played this deadlier game, the game that lay beneath the cards. Like a wary fencer he was feeling his opponent out, trying to divine the next attack in order that he could be ready with a riposte. He did not underestimate John T. Alsop.

73

The play was fast. Alsop stayed about even, perhaps losing a little. Ellis won some, not much. Dave held good cards from the first; and although he was playing with no more than half his mind, by instinct rather than by reason, and didn't press his luck, as ordinarily he would have done, he piled the chips high.

This did not cause him to crow. He knew the game too well. He was not averse to winning the first pot or pots, but he was never moved to excitement by this circumstance. Besides, he had something else on his mind now.

For the better part of a year, when it meant a great deal to him, when he was short of money, he had been staying even or at best a trifle ahead; but now that it didn't matter, for he had plenty of cash, he seemed to win no matter what he did. There was luck for you!

But—*was* it luck? Could it be that they were playing with doctored cards, and that Alsop and Ellis were dealing him good hands in order to cause him to win with suspicious promptitude? Such a maneuver could lead up to the moment when one of them, perhaps having planted a card on him, would suddenly and dramatically expose him as a cheat. If so, would Alsop then draw a gun and kill him? It was conceivable.

The pack of cards in Dave's pocket had been treated: the bartender's manner was proof enough of that. Could it have been merely an extra safeguard? Were the cards they played with now also marked cards? This did not seem likely. For one thing, Alsop presumably would not risk a long game with marked cards, which after all might be detected. Much more likely he would introduce a cold deck, previously treated by himself, only for the killing, toward the end of the game. And when would the game end? At Natchez? They were due to dock there soon. Senator Alsop had many friends in politically rotten Natchez-under-the-Hill, his headquarters. He could get out of almost any crime committed there—perhaps even murder, if there were any semblance of self-defense.

Dave felt a bit cold at the thought, and the skin at the back of his neck prickled. He pushed out some chips.

"Call and raise it five."

No, he did not believe that these cards had been prepared. His fingers were singularly sensitive, yet they could find no evidence of crimping along the edges. The aces and kings were exactly the same width and length

74

as the lower cards; that meant they had not been "shaved" to make them easier handling for a man who wished to deal seconds. Dave's fingers failed to detect any trace of spermacetti at the corners, just as his eyes noted no smear of color, howsoever minute, on the backs.

"I'll call you and raise another five, Mr.—uh—what did you say the name was, again?"

"Macdonough."

"Ah, yes, Macdonough."

Alsop's ice-blue eyes were fixed on him, but not in threat; the man was too astute to threaten openly. He studied David just as anybody drawing three cards might study a player who had drawn only one—wondering whether this was a bluff.

"Again," Dave said, pushing out ten dollars' worth of chips.

The senator sighed.

"Got to keep it honest," he said, and put up five dollars. "You fill?"

Dave nodded and showed his hand: a small straight.

A murmur rose. It was the biggest pot yet.

"Very pretty." Ellis smirked and leaned close to Dave Macdonough.

Was Ellis trying to see whether he had a pistol under his coat? Dave leaned forward as he raked in the pot. He moved the whisky flip on the table between him and Ellis. He had not sipped the drink.

Then the senator went into his act, almost like a vaudeville performer at the right cue. There should have been a roll of drums.

"By God, gentlemen, I've had enough of these cards!" He scooped up a handful and began tearing them in half. "I'm not superstitious, but—"

Then he appeared to recover himself. He apologized for the childish display of temper.

"Of course there was nothing wrong with the cards, only with me," he said. "Here, I've ruined these and I'm sorry. Let me get another deck."

He left the table, went to the bar and put down a coin. The bartender handed him the top deck but didn't get a chance to tell him what had happened. The players were all watching.

Still apologetic, and breaking the box open, the senator returned to the table. He extracted the joker, riffled

75

out the new cards, face down, then gathered them in and passed them for shuffling.

"Of *course* I didn't mean to imply that there was anything wrong with those other ones, gentlemen," he said again. "This is not that kind of game. I don't play cards very often, but when I do, by God, there's nothing I hate so much as a cheat!"

He was looking right at David, but he was smiling.

He's going to get a shock when he starts playing with these, Dave thought.

They were nearing Natchez. They knew this without looking out—knew it from the increased traffic, the number of boats that saluted them.

Covertly, Dave watched the senator. What was he going to do? He would change his plans when eyes and fingertips told him that these were not the cards he had touched up. Dave would have loved to tell him that *those* cards were in fact in his, David's, pocket.

But then he began to grow cold all over, as a new thought came to him. That prickling at the back of his neck increased.

They must be off Natchez now, for they had cut speed and were making for the east bank.

If Alsop intended to shoot he would shoot here. And he wouldn't need to plant a marked card on Dave—Dave already had a pocketful of marked cards! Alsop didn't know this, but the Natchez police would soon find it out. Dave also had two small pistols, both loaded. And there was Ellis, who undoubtedly would testify that it had been self-defense.

A very pretty case, a perfect setup. Influence or no influence, Alsop's lawyer would have little to worry about.

Unless, of course, it was Alsop who died and not David.

In any event, Dave must get rid of the cards he had in his pocket. He must do this right away. He would excuse himself to go to the privy, and dump them down the seat.

He rose.

"If you gentlemen will excuse me for a minute—"

The starboard deck door was flung open. A small pink-faced rabbit of a man with popping eyes stood there, the captain by his side. Behind them were two deck hands with horse pistols.

"There he is!" the little popeyed man squealed. "A

76

professional gambler! He's been exposed—I saw it myself! He's been—"

This must have been one of the *Tuscaloosa* passengers of two weeks ago, who had seen and recognized Dave through a window.

Alsop did not know this. Alsop thought that *he* was meant, that *he* had been betrayed. He sprang to his feet.

"Damn you, Macdonough, you turned me in!"

His right hand went under his coat.

Dave already was standing, leaning forward a little, both hands on the table. Out of a corner of his eye he saw Ellis move. Ellis might have meant to kick him or shove his chair against him—anything to throw him off balance while the senator got his gun out.

Dave tossed the whisky flip into Ellis's face. He did this with his left hand, while with his right he drew one of the Ketlands.

Alsop got out his gun. Dave fired.

He tried no trick shot. He was not showing off. He aimed at the surest target—the middle of the chest.

The Ketland, big-bored, double-barreled, carried a tremendous charge. It kicked high in Dave's hand. The air suddenly filled with smoke. The roar was ear-shattering.

John T. Alsop went backward, right over his chair, and crashed to the floor. Cards were strewn about him. He was screeching with pain.

For perhaps a second this was the only sound, this high thin screeching. Nobody moved. They might all have been petrified—the players, the customers, the bartender, the men in the doorway. Smoke swirled sadly among them. Whisky from an overturned drink dribbled to the floor.

Then Dave sprang toward the larboard door. He heard a shout from the other side. There was a terrific explosion —one of the horse pistols?—but he didn't pause to learn where the ball went.

Out on deck, he spun on his heel and raced toward the stern.

He meant to get below, to the boiler deck, the lowest and biggest deck, where the machinery was, the landing stages, most of the cargo, and of course the deck passengers. Where would you hide a leaf? In the forest. A shell? On the shore. Then what better place to conceal a man

77

than in a crowd? There would be a crowd on the boiler deck. There always was.

He skidded to a stop at the stern end of the boiler deck. The shot had been heard below, and dozens of passengers stood near the foot of that ladder, staring up. Sure, a crowd was what he sought! but not one in the open, not one that was all eyes, facing him. That afterdeck down there was in effect the second-class promenade. Splotched with spittle, bathed in the red light of the furnaces, stinking of sweat and cottonseed oil, it was the space the dainty ladies of first-class detested when they had to walk across it on the way to stairs that would take them to more comfortable quarters above. It was the place for jigs and brawls. It was not the place for David Macdonough right now.

Without hesitation he whirled around and started to run forward again, though he could hear them pelting aft toward him from the barroom. He had no wish to make Pennsylvania again—and perhaps be trapped in possession of that damning evidence—but if he could reach the nearest door he might find his way down to a dimmer section of the boiler deck, a covered place amidships, where at least he could catch his breath.

He ran toward a door. It was thrown open from the inside. Two officers appeared, one with a rifle.

Dave drew the second Ketland and fired with his left hand. It was a good shot. It smashed the hurricane lamp in a bracket above the officers' heads, putting out the light and showering them with glass, after which it skittered along the bulwark and the bottom of the texas deck alternately, knocking back and forth, ripping out splinters, making a frightful noise. The officers dodged back through the doorway. The crowd from the bar slid to a stop, scared.

Dave looked around. *Maid Marian* was in a calculated drift, paddles not moving, for they were just off Natchez now. The water between boat and shore was stippled with lights from both. He could try to swim it; but he was almost certain to be seen and picked up.

There was only one other thing he could do, and he did it. He climbed over the rail and onto the after half of the paddle box. Sideways, placing his feet carefully, he let himself down to the lowest part of the box, where it overhung the exposed paddles themselves. The paddles were not moving, but he had no way of knowing when

78

they might start. *Maid Marian*, large, new, could be assumed to have two engines, two seats of bearings, two stub shafts, mighty handy for landing purposes especially if the current was strong, whereby the paddles on one side could be turned one way while those on the other side could be turned the opposite way or held motionless. If this wheel started to turn while David was on it, he would be shredded like a coconut, pulped like a pineapple.

It would be necessary for him to lower himself down to the third wide wet wooden blade before he could even think of making a jump to the nearest boiler room port.

He let himself down to the first. It was slippery, and for a moment he teetered, catching his breath. Then he got his balance, and slid down to his chest and let his legs hang, feeling for the second blade with his feet. Feet in place, he worked downward.

As he slithered down over the second blade, both arms around it, letting the lower part of his body over the edge, he heard a series of bells from the engine room. The wheel began to tremble.

He found the third blade with his feet. He didn't feel it out. He didn't have time. He let go, turning.

He jumped.

It was a distance of about four feet, and with any kind of foundation to start from he would have made it easily. As it was, the wheel began to turn. The blade of course was wet. Dave missed the edge of the port with his feet, but he caught it with his hands, then slipped his arms over it, and for half a minute hung there, panting.

The wheel was going around now, going forward. The great thick oak blades slashed by David Macdonough, not a foot from his head.

After a while, carefully, he shinned up over the bottom of the port, a rectangular one, and dropped with no sound upon the boiler deck.

He should be near the middle of the boat now, in among the cargo.

The place was dark. He reached out. His hands met a piece of cloth. The cloth had flesh behind it.

Not two feet from his face a voice said, "That's a darn nice pistol you got there, mister. A Ketland, is it?"

Dave stood perfectly still. His eyes began to adjust and he saw that the gloom was not complete: some glow came from the afterdeck.

79

"What makes you think it's a Ketland?" he asked quietly.

"I like guns. Used to work for a gunsmith in Cincinnati."

"They don't make shooters like this in Cincinnati."

"Reckon it *is* a Ketland then."

"Yes. Would you like to own it?"

The man's voice was flat, toneless, a New England nasal. Dave could see him somewhat better now: an uncommonly tall fellow, a gangler, all joints and angles, slabsided, somber.

"What do you want me to do, mister?"

"Anybody else see me come inboard?"

"Don't know. Not likely. Folks're all back there watching us making to tie up. We're backing in."

"Yes," Dave said, and wondered what came next.

"That your hat? Dadhangingest one I ever did see."

The tall man gave a nod. Dave turned. In the water beyond the paddlewheel, in full sight, bathed in light from boat and shore, there rocked a mustard-yellow beaver. Dave was as amazed to learn that he no longer wore it on his head as a moment earlier he had been astonished to learn that a pistol still was in his hand.

A rifle cracked, probably from the texas, and the beaver bobbed wildly when a spear of water rose beside it. Then there was another shot, and another spear of water. Then another.

"There but for the grace of God—" Dave muttered.

He turned back to the tall man.

"I guess I'd better go ashore," he said.

"I got a place I can hide you," the man told him.

"No, I'd better go ashore. The Ketland's yours if you get me there."

The man scratched his chin. "Let's go forward right now. Safer."

Here was in truth a nether world, an underworld. Passengers were being shoved back from the afterdeck while hands made ready the landing stages. Grunting, greasy creatures, only half seen, they bumped one another softly in the darkness, like moths against a windowpane. They mumbled. They tittered. It was hard to think of them as human. There was something gnomelike about the way they glided from place to place, their eyes showing white.

80

To David's relief, they appeared to pay little attention to him.

His guide led him to a small triangular forward deck. It was deserted. He saw a few crates, a few packing cases.

There was no more than the usual confusion at the landing, but men with rifles moved everywhere, and lights showed on all sides. Everybody who went over the planks was scrutinized. A rat couldn't have plopped into the water unseen.

Physically Dave was only the length of *Maid Marian* from the city known as a sink of sin, from the celebrated gambling houses and bars and brothels of Natchez-under-the-Hill. He might just as well have been miles away.

The sentries even peered at a man who was carried off the boat on a stretcher, and who, Dave noted, still moaned.

"That your friend?" the Yankee asked.

Dave did not answer.

After they had backed out into the stream again, lights began to appear in the second tier of windows just above the place where Dave sat. The first tier, a deck with no walking space outside, was, forward here, the dining saloon. It stayed dark. But on the second tier, the promenade deck, was the ballroom, where an hour earlier he had watched Adoree wheel in the arms of that tall dark-eyed young aristocrat. *This* was fully lighted, and soon the musicians began to tune up.

Maid Marian, taking the middle of the stream, really went booming. The Yankee said the report was that the steamer, having taken on her full quota of passengers at Natchez, was going to keep right on booming clear to New Orleans.

"That'll give 'em a heap of time to search," he added.

"Search?"

"They're starting now. See them pips of light? Lanterns. They're combing every inch of the deck. Heading this way."

Dave sighed. He looked up at the promenade, the rail, the lights from the ballroom. The fiddlers were at it for fair now, and the shadows of dancers swung across the windows.

Dave handed over one of the Ketlands.

"All right," he said. "Now where's my hiding place?"

"Mister," the Yankee drawled, "you're sitting on it."

CHAPTER 11

THE SEARCHERS were tired. They had squirmed and elbowed their messy malodorous way from the stern, and by the time they reached the forward deck, the end of their search, they were inclined to be careless, no doubt convinced by then that the man who had shot Senator Alsop had somehow slipped ashore at Natchez, or been drowned trying. They pushed a couple of packing cases around. They kicked the crate Dave crouched in. They went away.

After a while the Yankee worked the top off the crate. He had literally nailed Dave in.

"Come on out," he invited. "Moon's rising. It's pretty."

David climbed out. The Yankee said his name was Weatherall and he proceeded to orient David as to future behavior. The agreement was that Dave remain on this little deck as much as possible, and be prepared to leap back into the crate at any time. The spot was uncovered, but the sky was clear. Dave's coat was mussed, his boots scuffed, his hands and face dirty, and he needed a shave. Weatherall found him somewhere a broad-brimmed black slouch hat. ("You look like one of them gold-rush men, heading for California!") That is, though he could not have stood a good inspection, he was safe enough in casual glances. With luck and the Yankee's help he might make it. He might even get ashore complete with carpetbag; or even if he had to leave the bag he could report its whereabouts to the men he worked for.

"You get me ashore in New Orleans, day after tomorrow," he said, "and I'll give you another Ketland, exactly like the one you've got."

"Say, mister, how many of those things do you carry?"

Weatherall was hardly friendly. He exuded suspicion, trusting nobody. He had the kind of face that seemed to be pressed against a barely-opened door, the kind of eyes that seemed forever squinting through a slit. Yet he was alert and conscientious. His humor was pawky. He seemed to know everybody. And certainly he had no scruples.

The only weakness Dave could detect in him seemed

commendable rather than otherwise: he was mad about pistols. He would talk pistols by the hour, until Dave, desperate, denied all other company, would close his eyes and pretend to be asleep. Later Dave would open one eye a little. The Yankee, still sitting on a barrel, would be turning the smart little Ketland over again, his face touched with devotion and even with awe, like that of a doting young mother who leans over her babe.

The next day was hot, and sensible men stayed out of the sun. Dave, aching from lack of exercise, his joints stiff, felt mighty unhappy on the small forward deck. Once he did go amidships, to rest his eyes from the sun's glare; but the stink of the place, the pounding of the engines, the low ceiling, the presence of so many of the unsoaped, drove him back to his crate. He was largely left alone. Weatherall, who mixed with the other passengers, and did not hover around his charge as he had the previous night, nevertheless did not lose touch with him. Weatherall reported that he saw nothing to indicate that another search was being organized.

Dave spent most of his time on his back, facing aft, watching the first class passengers as they walked the promenade. He saw Adoree time and again. She was chatty, gay, twirling a tiny lace parasol, while her skirt, flounced with point d'Alençon, bobbed and swayed on its hoops. This did not wound Dave, this attitude. He knew that a person in Adoree's position acted a part most of the time. Gaiety was an obligation.

Always Adoree was accompanied by a male, usually by that dark-haired young man Dave had seen as her dancing partner. Dave studied him. Tall, arrogant, handsome, he had about him an air of easiness; and when he leaned over Adoree he would put a hand on her forearm in a manner smugly possessive.

Dave decided that he hated the fellow, who could take his background for granted.

The only time Dave saw Adoree alone was on the second night, the night that was to be the last of the trip. She stood at the rail just above where he lay. She wore yellow, the yellow of buttercups, which must have brought out the cornflower blue of her eyes: he could not see them. Her bosom and arms were bare. An ivory fan dangled from her wrist. She wore no bonnet, and her fair fine hair was drawn back to a bun caught up in a net in which brilliants blinked.

83

It took the breath out of him to look at her.

He rose.

More than once he had eyed the space between where he lay and the rail of the promenade. A catwalk, presumably there for window cleaners, ran around the saloon deck just under the dining saloon and the catwalk could be reached by standing on a packing case. The windows themselves had substantial sills, while above them, extending as far up as the promenade rail, a fretwork of gilded wooden molding, purely ornamental, of a foliaceous design, offered a grip to any reasonably agile man.

The danger, the thing he worried about, was that he might be seen either by somebody passing on the promenade who chanced to look down, or else by somebody in the dining saloon.

But—a kiss would be worth it.

Getting up on the catwalk proved easy. He had a good four inches of shelf to stand on then. Raising his head, he peered through a dining saloon window. Dinner was finished but some diners remained. There was in particular one large party, wholly stag. Bottles were being opened.

Dave looked up. Adoree had not seen him. Elbows on the rail, she stared straight ahead, and there were tears in her eyes. The tears did not gush, just hung there glittering. Dave swallowed hard, and peeked into the dining saloon again.

Now he had a stroke of luck. A waiter with a tray of empty glasses, making for the kitchen door, was jostled by a drunken diner, who was making for quite a different room. The waiter saved about half the glasses, but the others made a lot of noise. Every head turned for a moment, but a moment was all Dave needed. Quickly he stepped to the sill, rose, grabbed the molding and worked himself to a position above the window. The footing here was by no means as firm as it had been on the catwalk. He paused to catch his breath. The steamboat vibrated, but not enough to disconcert him.

He climbed a little higher, until he was able to reach an upright of the promenade rail with his left hand. With his right hand he swept off the disgraceful black hat.

"Your servant, Miss Sanderson."

She did not scream, perhaps because she couldn't. He heard her breath sucked in, and caught a small sound from the back of her throat, but that was all—except that her hands tightened on the rail. The tears that had hung, crystal-bright, one in each eye, now broke and rolled down her cheeks. Even in that first split-second, before she lowered her head to look at him, Dave knew that she'd recognized his voice and that it filled her with joy.

"David! They said you'd been drowned—or shot!"

"I was lucky."

"But—I don't understand! Why did you walk right past me last night? Why were you—"

"There isn't time to explain now." He raised himself a little higher, so that his head just cleared the level of the deck. He saw that nobody else was in sight on the promenade or below. But this could hardly last. His voice was low, urgent. "Not any more than I can explain now being thrown off the *Tuscaloosa*. Tomorrow night maybe."

"Oh, that beastly *Tuscaloosa* captain! I'm going to speak to Uncle Jason about him!"

"He was only carrying out your Uncle Jason's orders," Dave told her.

She blinked, unable to comprehend. He had put his hat back on, and now he held one of her hands, the ivory fan swinging against his wrist, while with the other hand he held the rail.

"But how could you stand such insults, David! Why didn't you call him out?"

Dave all but smiled. The thought of stumpy John Wells marching forth to the field of honor tickled his fancy. At that, Wells would do a good job of it, the duello, as far as Dave could make out, being as much play-acting as fighting and maybe more. But Adoree had been serious. To her, a New Orleans aristocrat, pistols-in-the-morning was the natural solution of any disagreement among men.

He squeezed her hand.

"There isn't time now," he whispered again. "I ought to be hiding. But when I saw you I couldn't help climbing up for a kiss."

"David—"

"Remember your uncle's garden? Remember the Cherokee roses? You said then that you'd bet I'd rather be on the top deck looking down than on the bottom deck looking up. And you were right. But maybe I'll be up with you soon, Adoree."

"You will! I know you will!"

"And meanwhile—"

He stretched as high as he could. She leaned far over, her lips slightly open, her eyes closed.

And a voice said, "Ah, *here* you are, mademoiselle! You ran away!"

Unkissed, Dave sank. He even got below the level of the deck, though he had to bend far over to do so. He had nothing but the fretwork to cling to—with knees, toes, elbows, fingertips. Adoree had let her fan fall as she straightened, and Dave had caught this adroitly enough. He could not spare a hand, however, so he put it into his mouth.

"La, you should have protection at night on a vessel like this," he heard the male voice above say, "with gamblers and murderers romping all around!"

And Adoree's reply:

"The man who shot that Senator Alsop is not likely to be *romping* anywhere right now, Raoul."

"I daresay. He's probably at the bottom of the river. Still, he *may* be down on the boiler deck. After all, we don't know much about things down there, do we?"

"No," Adoree responded tartly. "And I can't say that I wish to."

Raoul had not come out on deck in order to discuss economic conditions among the suppressed classes. Looking up, Dave could see the tall man's hand slip over Adoree's hand on the rail. It was all that he could see of the two of them, though his head was only inches from their feet. Adoree tried to draw her hand away.

"Please, Raoul—"

"Oh, now, see here! I've been waiting for three days to—"

"*Raoul!*"

David Macdonough had no reason to boil. The fanciest genealogical background the annals of heraldry show won't keep a man from behaving in a certain way under certain circumstances. Given the dark, a deck, and a girl as desirable as Adoree, Dave himself might have done what Raoul did, or tried to do. Moreover, Adoree's own hand now reappeared at the rail, and it waved down, as if pleading with him not to interfere. Adoree was perfectly capable of taking care of herself. Beautiful women must learn to slap.

Here was the voice of common sense again. And as

before, Dave Macdonough ignored it. He acted on impulse. He rose, teetering, and reached an arm under the lowest horizontal of the rail. He seized Raoul's right ankle and pulled—hard.

Despite the unexpectedness of the attack, it could scarcely have succeeded so well had it not been assisted. Adoree just at the same instant was engaged in shoving Raoul on the chest. The combination of push above and pull below cost the tall young man his balance. He landed on his backside with a resounding thump.

Adoree shrieked with swiftly-suppressed laughter, and turned and ran away.

Dave, chuckling, the fan between his teeth, climbed spiderlike down to the boiler deck. As he passed the dining saloon he caught a glimpse of a drunken man stabbing a finger toward him: "Pirates! I saw one! He had a knife in his mouth!"

Lest Raoul lean over the rail, or somebody in the dining saloon open a window and look down, Dave stepped into the shadow of the covered part of the deck, the cargo space.

Soon Weatherall sought him out there. Weatherall was never far away. He wanted that other gun.

"I don't know what you've been up to, but anyway there's another search party coming. There's a heap of talk about pirates."

Dave sighed. He looked out at the forward deck.

"That's right," Weatherall said. "Back into that box!"

It was a long night, and a mighty uncomfortable one, yet most of the time, cramped though he was, and scarcely able to breathe, David Macdonough smiled and smiled.

Perhaps this second alarm had disgusted the overworked mates; or perhaps they did not truly believe the drunken passenger and his tale of pirates. At any rate, the search was a perfunctory one. And in the morning, with Weatherall's help, Dave was able to brush off, and wash, and get a good shave. When he went back up to Pennsylvania, a gentleman, he was not challenged. At New Orleans he walked off carrying the carpetbag. The purser even bowed to him. Gracious always, David Macdonough bowed back.

87

CHAPTER 12

THERE were no rough surfaces in the Martineau drawing room. Nothing there was dull. Everything gleamed—the floor, the frames of portraits that hung on the wall, the prism chandelier, the yellow-veined Numidian marble fireplace, the bronze clock figures of Freischütz and Agatha all enclosed in a glass dome. The Oriental rugs were strewn about with an air of Oriental lavishness. The woods were mostly dark strong hard tropical woods—mahogany, ebony, teak—yet the room was by no means dim. Its French windows gave upon a garden, the same small front garden, in which Dave had first met Jason Martineau's niece, a spot murmurous now with bees; while beyond that, beyond the fence and the hedge, there stirred all the bustle of Bourbon Street.

New Orleans! The city fascinated him. The rawness of the frontier was cheek-by-jowl with the elegance of the Old World here. Riverfront rowdies rubbed elbows with grandees from France and from Spain. Trappers, planters, bisque-faced Neopolitan fishermen, nuns, Negroes, tall severe Indians, sometimes too a Yankee like David Macdonough: most of these were passers-through. The real New Orleans was a small town, and one that tolerated no middle class, everybody there being either on top or at the bottom. Significantly, it was not contributing much to the Gold Rush. Dave did not suppose that he himself ever would be accepted in the City of the Crescent. If he met with success in carrying out the plan he was about to submit to the financiers, then he'd be acclaimed. This did not interest him, except as it might mean the opportunity to make more money. But even if hailed as a hero, he doubted that he would be accepted into New Orleans society. The Lafitte brothers, Pierre and Jean, had been almost a myth in their own time; yet though they strove mightily and their exploits were much applauded, their neighbors never did forget that they were the sons of a blacksmith. They might bow before well-born ladies encountered in the street, the Lafittes, but seldom did they get a chance to jackknife themselves over the hand of such a one in her own drawing room. They just weren't gentlemen, that's all. Neither was

Dave Macdonough. What could you do, he wondered to get to be a gentleman?

He heard a step behind him, and he turned to face one of the genuine articles. *This* man had never needed to work for his position.

His frockcoat, plum-colored, was high in the waist, his yellow trousers very tight, his mustaches exquisitely waxed. He was tall, dark, carelessly handsome, of age not much more than twenty. He carried an extremely long walking-stick with a gold knob. There were rings on his fingers, fobs at his silken waistcoat. He raised a quizzing glass, and through this regarded Dave.

"I don't believe I've had the honor of meeting you, sir?"

I knocked you on your tail last night, Dave thought. *Want another as a formal introduction?* But he didn't say that. What he actually did say, with a nod, was: "Name's Macdonough."

The young man bowed.

"Charvet, sir. Your servant. You are, uh, waiting for somebody, Mr. Macdonough?"

"Yes."

Suddenly, and with an abrupt change of attitude, his eyes flashing, brows low, Raoul Charvet said, "Not for Miss Sanderson, I trust?"

The mouth became tight, the lips curling back to display a hint of teeth. The man all but snarled, he who a moment before had been so amiable. His face had gone pale with rage. He seemed no longer to breathe. And this was not play-acting! He was dangerous, Dave decided.

"No," Dave said. "Her uncle, Mr. Martineau."

"Ah, of course!" Again Charvet was all graciousness. He might even have been unaware that this flash of rage showed, that his mask had slipped for a moment. "You have business with Mr. Martineau, no doubt?"

"Yes."

Now Charvet put himself out to please. He asked David how long he had been in New Orleans, and what he thought of the place. Through the window he identified various bushes, pointing with his cane, giving a history of each. He did everything he could to make David feel at home.

Dave was touched. One often encountered such open-handedness and immediate friendliness among back-

89

woodsmen, but in a dandy like this it must have meant a considerable effort. Perhaps because he had so few of them himself, Dave Macdonough always admired good manners. He scarcely listened to Charvet as the tall young man chattered, but he watched him with an attentive eye.

All this was changed when Adoree entered. She gave a glad cry at sight of David, ignoring Charvet's bow, if she saw it.

"David! I'm so happy! You—you're looking fine."

He was, and he knew it. His boots shone. He had bought a new beaver, a new cravat. He even managed a tolerably courtly bow.

Charvet straightened up from *his* bow, face taut with hurt pride. He had been made to look ridiculous. And indeed, what Adoree had done was not polite, as she herself realized, hastening to apologize.

"Mr. Macdonough is an old friend," she explained.

"Whereas me," said Raoul Charvet with a wry smile, "you always have with you."

The change in the young man was almost unbelievable. The voice trembled, despite an obvious effort to keep it light and flippant. The eyes flashed. The face, appallingly pale again, became beaded with fine bright sweat. The fingers twitched.

These signs, foreboding an outburst, clearly were familiar to Adoree Sanderson, whose uneasiness showed.

Dave, on the other hand, was enjoying himself. He bowed yet again.

"It is always felicitous to meet you, Miss Sanderson. It's especially so this afternoon, since it gives me a chance to return something you let fall the last time we talked."

He fished out the fan. He heard Charvet gasp. There wasn't the slightest doubt that Charvet recognized the fan. No doubt the fan had some special significance. Conceivably it had been a gift from him.

"Oh thank you."

Adoree was frightened, Dave could see that. Charvet started forward.

"Would it be too much to ask, Mr. Macdonough, where you—"

"Forgive me, here's my host. Business before pleasure, as we say up North. And it's not only Mr. Martineau. There's a whole horde of bigwigs waiting to see me in the library there. So—"

He bowed yet again before Adoree. He was getting good at bowing. Toward Charvet he inclined a curt head.

"Your servant, sir."

"Your servant."

Jason Martineau, that rich man, in matters of business could be a sphinx; but patently he was troubled as he led Dave across a huge hall toward the door of the library.

"I don't like that look on young Charvet's face. I hope you haven't offended him, Macdonough?"

"I hope not."

"You don't seem very frightened."

"Should I be?"

"Bluntly, yes. That lad's a bad one to cross, make no mistake about it. He's a crack shot and one of the best swordsmen in the city. He can't be brushed aside, he's too important. And in anything to do with my niece he's never quite in his right mind. I suppose it isn't his fault, really. He's infatuated. He's utterly consumed with jealousy."

"He keeps the others away?"

"He does! They're all afraid of him. And they have a right to be. In everything else young Charvet is charming, but when it comes to Adoree—well, I don't know what you were saying, Macdonough, just before I came in there, but I don't like that look on Charvet's face. You offend him, man, and there's no shillyshallying. You get a challenge right away. First thing next morning. It comes up with the coffee."

"Maybe I only seem calm because I've got something else on my mind."

"I like you, Macdonough. I wouldn't want to see anything happen to you."

"Well, for that matter, neither would I." Dave nodded to the library door. "But of two evils, let's choose the more complicated, eh? What I'm going to propose to these gentlemen isn't exactly a dance around the Maypole either."

These were men who knew what they wanted. David felt more at home with such folks than with the flibbertigibbets of the upper deck or the dregs of the lower. There was no false friendliness here, yet neither did the men seethe in suspicion. Already impressed—they

91

had the contents of the carpetbag spread on the table—still they wished to hear all that he had to say for himself. This was as it should be. If they were going to put their money into something they wanted to know all about it, just like the men where David came from. Finicky manners had no place in a business conference. On the other hand, there was no note of hostility. David never could understand why people spoke of "cold" bargainers. A bargain, any bargain, being an agreement, was by the very nature of it a warm thing.

So he felt relaxed, nodding right and left. He knew these dealers. They were the persons who really ran New Orleans. They stayed in the background, but they pulled the strings. Excepting the host and Judge Ryerson, none had been in on the fateful poker game aboard the *Tuscaloosa*, but they all had large holdings in steamboats. They had assembled around this same library table that night a month ago when Dave was hired, the night he'd gone for a stroll in the garden whilst awaiting their decision. They were the same men, now.

Ryerson made a great ado over Dave, pumping his hand. "By God, sir, you got that watch back! I can't tell you how much that means to me!"

"They'll get it away from you again, Judge," somebody said. "Nobody's watch'll be safe on this river—no, nor nobody's life either—unless we clean up Satan's Brood."

"By God, sir, that's absolutely right! And here's the man can do it for us! Sit down, David, sit down! And no matter what comes out of this meeting, sir, I want you to know that I am personally indebted to you. I want you to feel you can ask me any favor any time you like."

"Thank you," Dave said.

"Suppose you just tell us the whole story, from beginning to end," Martineau suggested. "Then give us your plan later."

This David did. He told a straightforward tale, omitting all mention of Sarah, whom he esteemed a personal problem, and ending with his departure from Buzzards' Roost. They must have deduced that he had come back aboard the *Maid Marian*, the only boat from the North these past several days, and they might well have wondered how. They could have learned, by a simple check, that there was no Macdonough on the passenger list, and of course they would have heard—it was all over town by now—that just off Natchez a professional gambler had been shot and seriously wounded by a passenger who subsequently disappeared. Doubtless they were making guesses as to the identity of that passenger. But they said nothing here. Businesslike, they stuck to business. The questions they asked him had to do with the location of Buzzards' Roost, its layout, its size, and the strength, number, and nature of the pirates who infested it. Dave's answers were precise. He had no written notes, but his memory was well stocked. The men were impressed.

Yet there was a snag.

"Mr. Macdonough, when you first appeared before us," one of the older ones pointed out, "it was with a promise to clean out this whole Augean stable yourself. You scorned assistants. We were to pay you ten thousand in gold if and when you had succeeded, plus your actual, itemized expenses, and that was all. But now you ask for a posse."

"Your pardon, sir, but I did not say that I'd clean it up alone. I'd never be as boastful as all that. What I did say was that I would go *in* there alone. I'd make a preliminary survey. Well, now we know."

"True—"

"There were two gangs, and one has wiped out the other. But the first one isn't going to be licked by any man alone. No, sir!"

"How large a party would you require?"

"Twenty men. Hand-picked by me. I could get them right here."

"How much would you have to pay apiece?"

"I don't know. Depends on how many are looking for a job. I'd give you a complete accounting in any case, of course."

They liked that. They nodded, leaning close.

Dave went on. If he was as yet uninformed as to the current daily wage for professional thugs, he did know the prices of guns, powder, provisions, and these he set forth in detail. The others at the table were well equipped to calculate the cost of transporting this band to the point of attack. For them, with their connections, the cost would not be great.

Dave also gave an estimate of the value of the property at Buzzards' Roost, aside from the safe and its contents.

"A heap of this," he added, "is represented by guns

93

and powder. Maybe the men could be paid off that way. Partly, anyhow."

"But—that would be looting!"

Dave looked at the man who had spoken.

"Why, yes, that would be looting," he agreed. "Do you seriously think you're going to keep men like this from looting anyway, no matter what happens? Why not take advantage of it?"

"M-m-m. You'd be there in person, of course, Mr. Macdonough?"

"I hope to be. But I may get trapped in the house."

"But—but—aren't you going to *lead* this tussle?"

"Not at first. I've got to go back to that place the way I first went there—alone. I'll give the men the most careful instructions possible, and then I'll go there all by myself."

"By God, man, that'd be putting your head into the lion's mouth!"

Dave nodded. "More or less, yes."

"But if you—"

"The sooner I get back there the better. They're going to be afraid I've skipped. They may skip themselves if they don't see me soon. And once they got into those swamps we'd never catch 'em. On the other hand, if I take back the money to account for this stuff," and he nodded to the booty on the table, "they'll think everything is all right. They'll get careless. And when the attack comes, they won't be ready."

"But where will *you* be?"

"I hope to slip out the night before, and join our men. We'll arrange a password."

"But what if you *don't* get out? You say the men will have orders to shoot to kill, and no parleying?"

"That's right."

"Then maybe *you'll* be killed by our own men!"

Dave shrugged. "I've thought of that. I reckon it's just one of those risks I've got to run."

"But see here, Macdonough, we'll be entrusting you, in that case, with a good-sized sum of money, cash."

"Are you implying, sir, that I—"

Judge Ryerson cut in.

"Nobody's questioning your honesty, David. All Mr. Albright meant was that in case you're killed and your body's frisked—which you yourself admit is possible—

then we'd be out the three or four thousand we advanced you for display purposes."

"You would," Dave conceded. "On the other hand, you would be in the ten thousand dollar fee, since I wouldn't be alive to collect it."

"But we'd give it to your heirs, we'd send it to your home!"

Dave rose.

"I haven't any heirs, and I haven't any home," he said. "All the same, I am as eager to get hold of that ten thousand dollars as you are to have me earn it. I won't let anything interfere. Are we agreed?"

They looked at one another, and nodded. They looked at him, nodding again. There was no need for a vote.

"Very good," Dave said. "Then I'll be about my recruiting." He made a bow. "Gentlemen, your servant."

Raoul Charvet was waiting in the hall, a highly unhappy young man. Dave sensed that Adoree had raged at him, had perhaps handed him his hat. Now he glowered at Dave.

"See here," he said, "I feel constrained to ask you where you got that ivory fan you gave to Miss Sanderson a little while ago."

Dave's thoughts were down at the waterfront. He shook his head.

"I don't feel constrained to tell you," he said. "Sorry."

He started past, but Charvet grabbed his left sleeve.

"See here, sir, I am not to be talked to in that fashion!"

"Then maybe," Dave said, "it'd be better to talk to you in *this* fashion!"

He punched Charvet on the point of the chin, hard. The young man slammed back against the wall. His eyes went glassy for a moment, then cleared. There was an expression of amazement in them, but no rage. He didn't lift his hands from his sides.

Dave watched him a moment, making sure that he was neither going to fall nor to fight. Then he shrugged and went out.

Half a square away, cursing himself for an impetuous fool, he turned back. He meant to apologize.

But the butler said that Mr. Charvet had taken his departure, adding that Miss Sanderson was locked in her room and not to be disturbed.

So Dave started again toward the river.

CHAPTER 13

MARTINEAU had been right. It did come with the coffee.

The bearer was a ramrod with prickly whiskers who introduced himself as Colbert.

"Won't you have some breakfast?" David offered. "I'll ring for another cup."

"Thank you, no, sir."

Colbert did not stir.

"Is this a challenge?" Dave picked up the note, put it down again, stirred his coffee, buttered a brioche. "Or aren't you supposed to know?"

"I have been asked to wait for a reply, sir."

"I'm afraid not. I never tackle correspondence in the morning."

"But this is—"

"I have other duties just now," Dave said firmly.

Colbert was conscious of the dignity of his position. Any person making arrangements for an affair of honor must be a model of decorum. The slightest touch of sarcasm, argument, exasperation, would defeat the whole purpose of the thing by lowering it to the level of the gutter.

So Colbert bowed. He placed a card on the table.

"You will of course answer this message. I assume as much."

"Oh, you do?"

"And of course it would not be proper for you to carry your answer in person, even to me, much less to my friend. But if the person you name will be good enough to bring it to me—at this address—good morning, sir."

"Not going?"

In the doorway Colbert turned to bow once again.

"I shall be home all day."

"I wouldn't," Dave advised. "It's too nice a day to stay indoors."

All that afternoon and half of that night he spent bent over nicked, stained, small tables back of riverfront and lower Canal Street dives, places reeking of gin and rum and rank tobacco, yet redolent with the memory of old-time toughs, of conspirators who had long since passed on to their fate; for now he was in the very incubator of revolutions and organized riots, the shops where violence was bought and sold. In whispers, hunched, alert, he interviewed a series of shifty characters. *They* came to *him;* for the previous night, after the conference at the Martineau house, David had gone among these same places passing out the word that he would have work of a certain kind for men who had sense enough not to ask too many questions. The grapevine had done the rest. They were waiting for him.

This particular labor market, it would appear, was glutted. The eagerness of many of the applicants was significant. Tall tales were told to David Macdonough, who peered through the murk at the tellers, nodding skeptically. Unparalleled feats of derring-do were described, others promised. There was nothing these cringers would not claim, lured by pay and the chance of loot. For the terms were good—fifty dollars and found for a job that shouldn't take more than a week, another fifty to the wife or accepted mistress if the man was killed. Who could ask for anything better than that? Dave Macdonough was fairly fawned upon.

Few paid any heed when he assured them that they would be sworn in as deputy federal marshals, a protection. They did not care what the fight was about. There was going to *be* a fight—that's all that mattered. Why drag the government into it?

In only one instance did Dave approach a man who had not approached him, and this was done half-playfully.

The sight of Weatherall, seated alone in a grogshop, morose as an owl, caught Dave's attention as he rose to go. He crossed to the man.

"Got a job yet? You wouldn't be interested in picking up a little fracas money, would you?"

"Not me," Weatherall said, not even looking around. "I went to a heap of trouble getting here, and here is where I'm going to stay. Coral your cutthroats somewhere else."

" 'The wicked flee when no man pursueth,' " Dave chided.

"Yeah," Weatherall agreed, "but they make much better time when they know somebody is after them."

Dave smiled. "I only thought that you might want a chance to try out those Ketlands," he said.

Now Weatherall turned, touching his pockets. He was drunk, red-eyed, but his voice was even.

97

"Mister, guns like these wasn't meant to be fired."

Dave shrugged. "Suit yourself." He started to turn away.

Weatherall put out an arresting hand.

"Speaking of pistols, what kind you going to use when you fight that man Charvet? I'd sure like to see them."

A punch in the pit of the stomach wouldn't have startled Dave more.

"I—I don't know what you're talking about."

"Sure you do. Surprises you, eh? Shouldn't. You don't know this place. I've only been here a day and a half, and I'm a dadblamed barbarian from the North to boot, but I get the gossip. You think a duel's a private matter, eh? Uh-uh. Not in New Orleans it ain't."

"I am afraid you've been associating with some irresponsible parties," Dave muttered, and strode away.

"Suit yourself," Weatherall called mockingly. "Still, I sure wish I could see them pistols. Think of me when you go bang, eh?"

Dave Macdonough signed up eleven of the twenty he needed, that night. They were the cream of hell. He went to bed feeling fine.

In the morning he again had breakfast in his hotel room. He liked that. He liked the languor of life here in the Crescent City, liked listening to the peddlers' calls in the Vieux Carré, and looking along streets so narrow that the balconies all but touched. He had never known a city like this. It had its eccentricities, which you had to accept; but by the Lord, eccentricities or no eccentricities, it certainly had charm!

He penned a note to Adoree Sanderson, asking if he might call on her this morning. He was signing this when Jason Martineau was announced.

Here was cause for amazement. Martineau, a banker, one of the biggest, in ordinary circumstances would not seek out an impecunious young adventurer in a ramshackle third-rate Old Quarter hotel. Something, clearly, was up.

"I am honored, sir. Have you had breakfast?"

"Yes."

Martineau still looked like a tired bishop with a talent for sarcasm, yet a glint of worriment showed in his eyes.

"See here, Macdonough, this Charvet affair is serious. It's damned serious."

"I had supposed," David said gently, "that such matters were private."

"In the rest of the world maybe. Not here." Martineau shook his head. "I'm not speaking as a representative of Southern chivalry, Macdonough. I'm speaking to you as a business man. You have undertaken certain obligations to me and my associates."

"Why, yes."

"It's a pity you had to offend Charvet, who's only too easy *to* offend, God knows. But what's done's done."

"I propose to apologize to him."

"You can't."

"Eh?"

"You assaulted him. It's not like a spoken insult. An insult you could explain, and if he chose to accept that explanation the matter would be dropped. But a blow can only be wiped out with blood. That's the way we do things down here. We may be wrong—I don't intend to argue about that—but anyway that's the way we do things."

David frowned. "You said something about business?"

"Yes. Personally I deplore this affair because I suspect that my niece is behind it, all unwittingly of course, and everybody else in town is going to jump to the same conclusion. She knows that herself."

"Miss Sanderson knows about this, uh, misunderstanding?"

"Of course. Maidenly ears hear a heap more than you might suppose, Macdonough."

"I had intended to call upon her this morning."

"I wouldn't. She's not receiving. It's better for her to stay under cover until the whole thing's finished."

"I'm afraid I don't understand."

"Damn it, Charvet sent you a challenge."

Dave nodded.

"And you haven't answered it," the banker pursued.

"I don't intend to answer it."

"*What?*" ·

"Of course not. As you yourself just pointed out, I have undertaken certain responsibilities. I've got a job to do. I can't let a silly little personal matter like this spoil my work."

"But that's just exactly what you *are* doing! Don't you see?"

"No, I don't see."

"Let me put it another way. I assume you've been recruiting, as you said you were going to?"

"I have. I've signed up eleven so far."

"Now, do you think you'll be able to sign up any more, or do you think that even those eleven will stay with you, once the word gets out that you've refused to accept a challenge?"

"I haven't refused to accept it. I've simply refused to acknowledge it."

"It comes to the same thing."

"Do you mean to tell me that those—those vermin I talked to last night have any interest in this matter?"

"They most certainly have. I'm afraid you're missing the point, Macdonough. We of the upper classes, here in New Orleans at least, are utterly dependent upon the lower classes. I hate to admit that but it's true. In any other place the *canaille* can look up to those slightly above them, who in turn look up to those slightly above *them*, and so-forth. But that doesn't apply here. There's nobody in between, in New Orleans. The consequence is, we're performing directly for the riffraff, for their benefit, just as if we were on a stage. No matter how much we may strut and what fine clothes we may wear, we're their servants—exactly as any actor is the servant of his audience.

"Now your plebian here, happens to like the duello," Martineau went on. "It fascinates him—all the pomposity of challenges and acceptances, arrangements, the cartel, the meeting, the bowing, everything rigid, everything proper. It's an act he calls for again and again, and we've got to give him what he wants. I am myself convinced that too damned much dueling goes on here. I've lost some good friends that way. I've had to go to the field myself, more than once, and risk everything I'd spent years building up, just because some harebrained whippersnapper saw fit to call me out. What's more, the whole system is forever spoiling business arrangements. I hate it. But I can't ignore it—and neither can you."

Dave went to the window. He stood a while gazing down at the street. A queer place, New Orleans, somewhat mad.

"I see what you mean," he said slowly. "They wouldn't follow me. Wouldn't even listen. But—would they hear about it, before we go?"

"Sure to. New Orleans is one vast whispering-gallery.

Besides, Charvet'd post you. You know what posting means?"

Dave nodded. He had heard of the practice. If a challenge were not accepted, the challenger could put a "card" in the newspapers, a paid advertisement, and in addition might paste actual posters all over the city, notifying readers that So-and-So was an arrant coward and a miscreant who had no respect for the principles of honor, an outcast thereafter from the society of decent people. A man who had been posted could never live it down. All he could do was pack up and move.

"He'd do that?" Dave asked wonderingly, watching a beturbaned, monstrously fat peddler of pralines. "He really would?"

"He most certainly would. I know that young man. I have no doubt that the piece is already in the hands of the printer."

The praline peddler was locked in lazy argument with a long lugubrious octaroon who wore two hats. A penny was involved. The argument might go on for hours. Why not?

"I could get killed," Dave pointed out. "I don't so much mind getting killed, but when that happens I want it to be for something I really hate—or love. I want it to mean something."

"Your attitude is understandable. Lots of us have felt the same way. But I don't see what you can do about it."

"Could I contend that I haven't any friends here?"

"I'm afraid that wouldn't hold water. I'd offer to represent you myself except for the fact that the offense occurred in my house, not to mention the additional fact that everybody believes my niece to have been the real cause of it. That puts me in a somewhat delicate position, as you can see."

"I suppose so."

The quarrel about the penny was waxing warm. A broom seller and a cadaverous character with enormous cavalry mustaches had recently joined it; and this being a big enough group to block the street, others were drifting to a stop. There was plenty of time.

"Do you think Judge Ryerson might act for me?"

"I haven't the slightest doubt that he would. He, uh, he's very fond of you, Macdonough."

"Suppose we go ask him. And if he agrees with you," Dave added with a sigh, "then I'm afraid I'm in for it."

101

They went, and asked.

The judge hesitated not a moment.

"Thank God you've come to your senses, lad. I was worried about you. Not your physical courage! I was worried about your common sense. Sometimes you don't seem to have much."

Dave gave a wry smile. "Different folks have different ideas about what common sense is, I guess. Well anyway, what do I do now?"

"I'll get dressed and go over to your hotel with you and we'll write an answer to that challenge. *You'll* write it, I'll dictate."

"The sooner the whole thing's over with the better."

"Sure. I see no reason why we can't pull it off tomorrow morning."

"One thing more," Dave said as the three of them were about to set forth. "Since I'm the one who's challenged, I can name the weapons. Right?"

"Why, of course. I'll lend you my own, if you want. Oscar Eggs. Damn' fine pistols."

"I don't happen to want pistols."

"Eh?"

"I want it to be with swords."

They were flabbergasted, their mouths open, eyes bugged out.

"But—but—you must be mad! Why, Charvet's the best swordsman in the city! Epee, foil, saber. He spends at least two hours every single afternoon at Senac's Academy."

"So I've heard tell."

"Can't you—it doesn't seem possible—but can't you shoot?"

"Oh, I can shoot all right," Dave said.

"Well, are you so good with a sword then?"

"Never had one in my hand. I wouldn't even know how to hold one."

"Why Charvet'd carve you to bits, man!"

"Now, *would* he?"

"Eh?"

"Think it over. I'm not interested in killing Charvet. I'm only interested in coming out of this business alive. Now suppose we meet with swords, and he sees right-off that I don't even know which foot to put forward? All right: That means he would do one of two things. He'd either run me right through—squosh!—or else he'd play with me for a while, make a fool of me, just to show off. But if he did that—and I can't help thinking it's what he most likely *would* do—then you don't suppose he'd be cold-blooded enough to run me through, do you? No. He'd probably finish the thing off by pinking me in the forearm. That would make him feel like a hero—and I could get bandaged up and go back to my job."

They thought about this a little. But Martineau shook his head.

"Charvet's not really sane. If he didn't come from such a good family he would have been locked up long ago. I wouldn't put anything past him. He's caused my poor niece all sorts of embarrassment. No, Macdonough, I admire your courage but I don't approve. It smacks of suicide."

"I agree, sir," Judge Ryerson said. "After all, David, this business involves my own honor as much as it does yours. I can't afford to be a party to a farce. It just wouldn't be right."

He put his hands on Dave's shoulders.

"And besides all that, lad, I think you've got a better chance of coming out alive if you shoot."

Dave fetched a sigh. He swallowed, a difficult thing to do.

"All right," he muttered. "Let's get that answer written then."

CHAPTER 14

THEY went in a hired coach, the windows rattling. Judge Ryerson had several carriages of his own, but his family's arms, emblazoned on each, were familiar sights in the city; whereas this meeting, theoretically at least, was a secret.

"Nervous, lad?"

"Yes."

"You don't look it. That's the important thing—not to look it."

The morning was misty, the air cold—a damp penetrating cold. Narrow though the streets were, the travelers could scarcely see the white-and-yellow houses they passed.

103

"Good God," the Judge cried suddenly. "I almost forgot! You aren't wearing flannel underwear, are you?"

"No," David said. "Why?"

Ryerson leaned back, exhaling in relief.

"Clean forgot to warn you. Damn' careless of me."

"Why?" Dave said again.

"It infects, that's the reason. Many a man's died of blood poisoning even after a surgeon has pried the ball out of him, just because some scraps of flannel got carried on in with it. Well, I guess you're all right then. That coat's fine."

"It's the only one I've got."

"No handkerchief showing—good. You're allowed to put your collar up if you ·wish, but you won't need it. That cravat will cover the white of your shirt when you're turned sideways. You don't want to offer any sort of target, y'see." His hand felt Dave's neckpiece, scarcely visible. "Ah, that's good too. No diamond."

"I don't own a diamond."

"But what's this? No flower in your buttonhole?"

"Is that so important?"

"It certainly is!" He reached out and tapped the coachman. "Stop here! Preston Poulet's house," he explained to Dave. "I know him well enough. Just a minute."

When he returned, mist swirling away from him, he pinned a small white flower on Dave's left lapel.

"There! Now you're fit to fight. Might look as if you were nervous, if you'd forgotten to wear a buttonhole. It'll be turned away from Charvet in the field, of course, so it's no target."

He settled back, relaxing, as though the greater part of his worries were past. David smiled in the darkness.

"Maybe I shouldn't make all this fuss," the Judge said after a while, "but somehow it's sort of part of the business. Men get more and more formal as they get more and more afraid. It gives 'em something to do, to keep their mind off what's coming."

"It would take more than just a flower to take my mind off it," David said.

"It's very pretty, that Cherokee rose." Ryerson looked out the window on his side. "It'll be light soon, and then this damn' fog'll go away—or should. You never get any reflections there under the oaks."

They were out in the country now. The Judge talked on, like a man afraid to face silence.

"I'll just review the rules for you though you'll hear 'em all on the field, of course. One shot each. Afterward, if you're not hit and if you are willing to apologize for the original offense, Charvet's bound to accept. I insisted upon that. And twenty paces. What's more, *I'll* do the pacing myself—and I've got long legs."

"I hope," Dave ventured, "that you didn't give Colbert the impression that I was shaking in my boots."

A hand smacked his knee.

"Lord love you, laddie! Why, the way I talked he thinks you're the sparks-spittingest, leather-hidedest, brass-bottomedest fireeater that ever was rowed up Salt River. Why, I pleaded with Colbert for twenty paces because I said there was some slight chance that you might miss at that distance. But it was sure murder at less, I said. I told him I knew for a fact that you had killed at least four men in duels up North, one shot for each. I said everybody in St. Louis was talking about you. I said you couldn't call out anybody up there any more—they were all too scared."

"How much of this do you suppose Colbert believed?"

"Hard to say. But it doesn't do any harm." The hand squeezed his knee. "You started it yourself, David, when you treated Colbert in such an offhand manner. It impressed him. You're a good poker player, David, and that's one reason why I'm not worried about you this morning. Dueling's a lot the same. It isn't all bluff—I don't mean that! But everything *else* being equal, the good bluffer will win."

The carriage left the road, clunked over spongy soft ground for a little, stopped. Judge Ryerson sprang out.

"Well, here we are. And we seem to be the first on the field, so that gives us the choice of position. Come along, laddie."

The live-oaks were enormous, the biggest trees Dave ever had seen. They were bearded with Spanish moss, and the mist squirmed among them, blurring their outlines, blocking off their tops.

"Les Chênes d'Allard," Judge Ryerson announced. "My friend Ned Allard owns all this property around here. You know—the poet."

Dave did not know, but he didn't answer.

The Judge paid the coachman, but asked him to wait.

105

"He would anyway," he added cheerfully. "And of course he's been followed."

Dave shivered. "You mean we're going to have an audience?"

"Bound to. But they'll stand far back. Afraid of being winged. Now, we'll establish the line of fire parallel with the bayou here—by the Three Sisters."

The Three Sisters were live-oaks neatly spaced along the edge of the bayou, each with its lower limbs higher than most.

"We'll place you at this end, so's you'll turn past the bayou and won't see anybody. You won't have to worry about reflections from the bayou itself."

No, Dave thought. It would be impossible to imagine anything less mirrorlike than that sad sheet of water. Had it not been for the sedges in the shallows he wouldn't have known where land left off and lagoon began. You could see only a few yards. This might have been a mill-pond; it might have been the Gulf.

"The Three Sisters," Ryerson rambled on. "They're called Aggie, Mabel, and Becky. Nobody knows why. You stand here. I hear—excuse me!"

So Dave stood alone, gazing at the live-oak. Tempted, he sneaked a look. He made himself whistle quietly, and pretended to adjust a bootstrap, while he glanced around.

The size of the party amazed him. There must be seven or eight men there. Raoul Charvet was remarkable as the tallest. He removed a long cape, languidly handing this to a friend, together with his beaver. He adjusted the flower in his buttonhole.

This was as much as David saw. It did not dismay, but rather irritated him. Why was *he* left alone like this? Should he be penalized for being on time?

Ryerson appeared with a case of pistols.

"Here they are. Pick 'em up, if you want. They're not loaded. We're going to load them right now, Colbert and I."

They were beautiful weapons, long, heavy, sleek. Made of unpolished Circassian walnut and blued steel, they had nothing about them that would gleam. They lay snug on red velvet. The name of the maker was on a silver plate on the under part of the lid, but it meant nothing to David. It was a French name.

"All right," he said.

"You don't want to snap 'em?"

106

"No."

"When they're loaded and I hand you one, be sure to hold it perfectly straight up. The charge'll be tamped in well but there's no sense taking any chances of loosening it. You can cock it then if you want, or you can wait for the signal. But remember—they're hair-triggered!"

"I'll remember."

"And whatever you do, don't start to turn before he says 'three!' Colbert has a right to shoot you if you do. Fact, it's his *obligation*, just as it's mine to shoot Charvet if *he* does."

"I won't start too soon," Dave promised.

"Here's Mr. Watts arriving. He'll give the count. In English, not in French. That's agreed. He's done this sort of thing before."

"Were you ever there when he did it?"

"No. But I've asked around. I was just going to bring that up. From what I hear, Watts has a habit of counting 'one' and 'two' slowly, and then after a long pause he says 'three' and then 'fire' quickly, one right on top of the other. You know, of course—we've been over this—you know you can start turning when he says 'three' but you mustn't shoot until he says 'fire.' But *probably* he'll say those two last words fast—'three-fire'—like that. *Probably.* Now I've got to go and do the pacing, so's Charvet can be put into position."

David blew out some breath. "It's about time," he said.

"Tut, lad, you're not nervous, are you?"

"Well, not any more'n I was before."

Ryerson touched his arm. "I'll be back soon. Think of other things."

Dave Macdonough stood there staring at that tree for a long time. He was aware, though he couldn't have said how, that a crowd was silently gathering. To the right he could make out vague figures in the mist. He did not try to count these, for he didn't wish to strain his eyes. He heard little, and what he did hear had a curiously muffled quality. Such voices as reached his ears were hushed, and they were mostly Ryerson's or Colbert's. These two were pacing the distance. Then they took an unconscionable while, it seemed, pouring powder, clipping wads, cutting lead. Dave could hear the ramrods squeal. He could hear the snap of molds, and even the squeak of the tiny scales on which the balls were separately and most scrupulously weighed. He shivered, standing so still. He fingered a certain suspender buckle in his pocket, turning it over and over.

Judge Ryerson came to him again. He was holding one of the pistols muzzle-up. He held it very carefully. He handed it to David, who took it in his right hand, still holding it upright.

"God bless you," Ryerson whispered, and disappeared.

A voice David had never heard before now started to speak. "I'll review again the rules agreed upon. From where I stand I will call 'one,' then 'two,' then 'three,' and finally 'fire.' You may cock your pistols at any time, gentlemen, but you must not move until I have said 'three.' Then you may start to turn. But you must not shoot until I have called 'fire.' Is that clear, gentlemen?"

"Quite," drawled Raoul Charvet.

"Sure," David said.

"Very well. *One!*"

With his right thumb Dave cocked the striker. He held the pistol close to his right ear, and the sear made a startlingly loud sound when it fell into place.

"*Two!*"

The mist was clearing. There was hardly a trace of it in the tree, and it slunk away low across the lagoon like a dog that has been whipped.

All the world was hushed, waiting.

"*Three—fire!*"

David Macdonough's first thought as he turned was that Charvet seemed such a long way off. He guessed he had never stopped to figure how far twenty paces were.

His next thought was that the fog had returned—returned with a rush, flooding the air, blotting everything from sight. And even as he realized this he felt something shove him in the left shoulder.

He was turning when this happened, and still bringing his pistol down. "Please don't push," he said.

The cloud cleared, wafted away by a breeze off the water, and he saw with a start that the stuff hadn't been fog at all, but gunsmoke.

Charvet had fired mighty fast. Why hadn't Dave heard the shot? Excitement? His nerves?

That shove. That must have been a ball, not a person. He'd been wounded then. He did not feel anything.

He went on lowering his pistol.

Raoul Charvet knew by now that he had missed, but he did not flinch. He did not lower his right arm, though he bent the elbow a bit. He raised the pistol before his face. A wisp of smoke dribbled out of the muzzle.

Dave had his pistol in line now. Through the sights his eye held a spot low in Charvet's chest. He grunted thoughtfully, feeling his power—the power of death. Then deliberately, he tipped the muzzle up, and fired.

Charvet, rigid, pale, did not move. Through the smoke a couple of leaves, shot off the tree just above his head, rocked a leisurely way to the ground.

Dave dropped the pistol.

"All right," he said. "Now I'll apologize."

CHAPTER 15

You might have supposed, to see them at the Martineau house, that they were celebrating some successful sporting event—as in a sense they were. It was an impromptu meal: coffee and cornbread, cold chicken, cold turkey, potato salad.

"But will they be up?" Dave had asked.

"*Up?* Lord love you, David, they most likely never even went to *bed*," the Judge had cried. "They wouldn't keep candles lighted, for fear of showing everybody how much interested they were. That wouldn't be proper. Do you see?"

"I suppose so."

"All the same, I'll bet Jason Martineau hasn't slept one wink. No, and what's more I doubt that his niece has either. We tut-tut and pooh-pooh in public, David," the Judge had added, "because that's the way we're supposed to act. But we don't always feel that way."

Another cold item was champagne. There were only six of them—the surgeon, the man who had called the signals, and the man who had lent the pistols, besides Mr. Martineau, the Judge, and David—but Jason Martineau unhesitatingly ordered the servants to open three bottles. Martineau, in high spirits, slapped Dave on the back. For Dave was one of them now, not an outsider, not an applicant for a job. Dave had fought his duel. He belonged to New Orleans. He was a member of the club.

There was a great deal of difference in the way they

treated him. He felt it. The attitude perhaps was childish; but as Mr. Martineau himself had said, it was the way they did things there.

They were proud of him. They beamed upon him.

"Long time since you've had wine this early in the morning, eh?"

Dave nodded, gulping. "No, I never had it—as early as this."

He might have added that he had never before had champagne at all, at any hour, but he refrained.

"Regular hunt breakfast, damn it," Judge Ryerson cried.

"Tell me about it again," begged Mr. Martineau, the only one who had not been there.

"Well, sir, Charvet was fast as lightning. Had his shot almost before David here was full around. Nicked him on top of the left shoulder, just barely enough to break the skin there. That proves he wasn't all the way turned. But David didn't move. And Charvet must have thought he'd missed. Shocked him. He isn't used to missing."

"I wasn't even sure I'd been touched," Dave murmured. "At first I thought somebody had come up and shoved me. But I was too busy taking aim to care."

"Then David had a perfectly clear shot, and he took his time, and his hand was a steady as a rock. He waited a couple of seconds that way, and then he was careful to shoot just above Charvet's head. It was damn handsomely done, I tell you! And then he turned around and made a first-rate apology. High-class, clear through. Charvet couldn't help but accept it. Even if that hadn't been set out in the cartel, he couldn't have done anything less. And I will say," Judge Ryerson finished, "he stood his ground like a man, while David here was drawing a bead on him. Didn't quiver."

"If he'd moved I probably would have killed him." Dave rose, looking around. "Excuse me—"

"Right at the head of the stairs," Martineau said.

Dave was a trifle dizzy as he crossed the room, making for the hallway. He told himself that it was the wine, though released nerves might have had something to do with it.

He parted the portieres, stepped out into the hall—and all but collided with Adoree Sanderson. This was still early in the morning, and the lady didn't have much on. Obviously she had been eavesdropping. Her eyes shone

110

with happiness and relief, yet there were tears in them too. It startled him, to see those tears. There was no reason, of course, why an aristocrat shouldn't be human; he had just never thought of Adoree Sanderson as a woman who would weep.

He said, "Oh."

"David, you're safe!"

"Yes."

"I know it's what womenfolks must put up with, and sure I wouldn't beg you to bend your honor—but—but—"

"Well, I'm alive anyway."

"And now you're one of us. I—I'm proud of you, David."

It sounded a mite prim. He cocked his head, regarding her quizzically.

"Now see here," he said suddenly, "I'm getting a little tired of being treated as if I'd just grown up and proved myself a man. I fought a duel, sure, and it was a damn-fool thing to do. But as far as being a man's concerned, why I think I've been one before this and I hope I'll be one again."

"Of course, David! It isn't that."

"Well, it sounds mighty like it."

"It's just that—well, down here people look at things like that different. You belong to us now. You're part of us. You're not a Yankee any more. You're a New Orleansian."

"All because I got up early in the morning and stood still long enough to let a conceited young dude take a shot at me."

"Well, yes. But there's more to it than that. I hope you're going to stay here, David. In New Orleans."

He stared at the stairway.

"Got a job to finish first," he said.

She clutched his lapels.

"Then it's true, what I overheard Uncle Jason say. You're going to organize this expedition and you're going to go back into that pirate camp all by yourself?"

"Yes, it's true all right."

"*Must* you do that, David?"

"Yes," he said, "I must."

She leaned closer. She swayed.

"But—but if—"

He took her hands away from his coat. He knew that he could never explain to her why he was going to

111

plunge back into the swamp. She had her ideas of honor and they didn't make much sense to him, and he was sure his ideas on that subject wouldn't make sense to her.

"I started the job and I've got to finish it, and that's that," he said. "Excuse me."

When he came downstairs again she wasn't there.

Fists on hips, feet spread, David surveyed the squad. For no good reason, memories of boyhood dreams about Robin Hood churned through his mind. Merry men, eh? *These* sure weren't! Glum, grim, grimy, they slouched. Nor were they garbed in anything like Lincoln green. Two wore buckskin, but the only word descriptive of the costumes of the others would be "nondescript." So far as they had any color, it was an oily gray. "Swamp clothes," one had said. "That's what you wanted, ain't it?" It was.

No delight filled Dave Macdonough as he looked upon these ruffians, but he was satisfied. He was getting what he'd bargained for. This was dirty work, and these were the dirty men to do it. If they stank, each was a dead shot; and despite the dismal appearance they presented, each, temporarily at least, as a deputy marshal, embodied in his unsavory person the might and majesty of the government at Washington.

"Well, you know your orders," he said to the ten who were to be dropped. "Make a camp and stay there tonight and tomorrow, to give the others time to come down from the north. Morrissy's got the map, and I want you to all take a good look at it, in case you get separated. Tomorrow sundown you start into the Brood. You keep going all night, until you come to Hogbelly. You can cross to it easy enough, wading. And you'll know when you've reached it."

They nodded lackadaisically, looking the other way.

"Them bodies still hanging there?" one asked.

"I expect they're not much more than bones by this time," David said. "Now at Hogbelly you ought to meet up with the other ten men, the ones that are coming south. And I ought to be there myself. I *hope* to be. Don't forget the password—'Tuscaloosa.'"

"Kill anybody that don't know it?"

"Absolutely!"

"What if the others ain't there?"

"I'm coming to that. Wait for them, and for me, until one hour before dawn. Then if we haven't come, you start

112

back for this house I told you about. Surround it. And don't let anybody leave it alive."

"Make a rush?"

"I wouldn't. There's only eight men, and you ought to get two or three at the first splatter, before they know you're there. Starve the rest out. You've got food for five days."

"What if they got food too?"

"They haven't."

"Burn the place?"

Dave shuddered at thought of all that gunpowder.

"That'd get 'em out all right," he conceded. "Trouble is, it'd leave you nothing but your pay."

It was a point well taken, and they nodded.

"But anyway, I hope to be with you by that time, and I'll make up your minds for you."

They were gathered on the boiler deck, at dusk. Dave knew that somewhere in that tangled mass the pirates of Buzzards' Roost were studying this boat. It could be that Sarah herself had the glass fixed to her eye, and was squinting at him, not knowing him, this very instant. Unless of course they had already wreaked their rage upon Sarah . . .

There would be no stop here. The steamer would come close to the east bank—so close that the Buzards' Roost men could see no more than the tops of her stacks, if that—and there, while still moving, discharge a raft with the ten men, the southern squad. Then the boat would enter Satan's Brood.

What were they thinking, up there? He believed he knew. They were wondering whether Captain Flambeau would be aboard this boat. They were wondering whether the boat would risk the run at night, and whether if it did they should attack, not waiting for the return of their leader. After all (they might well be telling one another), this here now Captain Flambeau, just when did he ever lead us against a steamer? And what reason have we got to think that we'll ever see him again? We were damn' fools to let him go off with all that jewelry. Well, we'll take it out on the girl. That'll be something to pass the time away. We ought to be able to make it last for days, we do it the way Cateau says. Maybe even a week.

"Let's heave that raft over," Dave commanded. "Only two things again: *Don't light a fire*, and *Don't let any-*
113

body get out of that house alive! That's all. Now get going—and God bless you."

The entrance into the Brood, as it had been when Dave stood with Adoree on the deck of the *Tuscaloosa,* was dramatic. It was an even more abrupt change in the case of this steamer, *Shreveport Belle,* since the entrance coincided with the setting of the sun, and darkness came suddenly with a rush, as if night were eager to reclaim with one swoop a place always properly hers. The passengers gasped, experiencing the sensation of persons who have entered a strange and utterly dark room, the door of which is closed behind them. Engine room bells rang furiously. Stewards scurried around lighting lamps.

Indeed, the number of lamps aboard this boat was extraordinary. They seemed to be everywhere. Also, there were men with pine-knot torches that spluttered and hissed, along both sides of the boat. The skipper, in this case acting on secret orders, was taking no chances. The men who held torches, and the men between these, were armed with rifles. On the boiler deck too, the engineers and stokers who were not actually on watch equipped themselves with long large weapons and posted themselves in conspicuous positions.

The pirates would be watching. Unblinking, motionless, like wildcats perched in trees, they would gaze upon this from out of the jungle.

They probably would see Dave Macdonough jump into the river. He certainly hoped they would.

His own remaining ten, the northern squad, which was to be slipped ashore just before daybreak at the upper entrance of Satan's Brood, had been pressed into service as boat guards, showing their guns. Dave passed among them, reminding them of the password, repeating all instructions.

"If I get there, all right. If I don't—well, that's too bad. See?"

They nodded again.

He shook hands with the captain. He slipped to the extreme stern, and when a brawl started up forward, causing heads to be turned that way—a contrived brawl, well timed—he caught his breath, held his nose and stepped off.

The river was cold. "Seeing's I've been in *hot* water so much lately, I suppose I ought to be pleased," he

114

told himself. His hat, the new beaver, bobbed near him. He retrieved it.

He watched the steamer's stern, fearful lest somebody not in the know, having seen him jump, might raise an alarm. Nothing of the sort happened. The *Shreveport Belle* slid slowly on, its lights ablaze, and got smaller, and smaller, and in a few minutes, having rounded a turn, she disappeared. David Macdonough, shivering, had the river to himself.

He swam in a feeble haze of moonlight.

Some time after he first felt mud under his feet, he at last dragged himself to comparatively dry land. The swimming and wading had tired him. He sat on a log, teeth chattering. He took his boots off.

There was no longer sign or sound of the steamer, no smoke from her stacks, not even the thud of engines. The last little wavelet from her wake had long since batted itself to rest.

The log on which Dave sat could hardly have been more than a few yards from the spot where he had first landed a month ago, and been called on by the scarecrow. He had planned this with care.

He took off his hat.

There was a dry whirr in the air near him. His head became a porcupine, and the water that clung to him seemed to turn to ice. He believed that his heart had stopped.

Something landed on the ground near him, something large and awkward. There was a low, sibilant sound.

Then he saw it—a buzzard. He had never known that they flew at night. They were bad enough in the daytime. This one squatted, all hunched wings, and surveyed him with an untroubled impersonal stare. He could see its dirty bare skinny wrinkled neck, its bald head, the redness of its tiny eyes. The buzzard waited. Buzzards do a lot of waiting.

Dave Macdonough shook his head. "You're too early," he whispered.

The bird did not stir.

Abruptly angry, Dave made as though to throw his hat at it. "Get the hell out of here!" he said.

The bird lurched upright and with an enormous effort spread enormous wings. It seemed to creak and squeak, as if its joints needed oil. Again there was that dry whirring sound. Ponderously, very slowly, as if not

115

sure whether it could do it, the bird rose into the air but only a little distance. With laborious heavy strokes it made its way to a spot fifteen or twenty feet up the beach, and there it settled, again hunching its wings high like a nasty-tempered old woman settling into a chair, and again gazing at David.

"You sure took your time," said a voice behind him.

He turned, to see Jake Lingle lounge out of the shadows of the swamp. Dave hadn't supposed, previously, that he would ever be glad to see Lingle. But he was.

"It's not as easy as you might think," he snapped. "They're guarding the boats mighty carefully these days. You saw that, just now. I had to come deck passage."

"Too bad."

"And I'm cold. Take me to the house. I want to get to bed."

"You'll find it's been kept warm for you."

That was how David knew that Sarah was still alive. He had not dared to ask. Asking would have been a sign of weakness.

"Keep close to me," Jake said. "Wouldn't want you to get lost."

Sarcasm twanged far back in that voice. These outlaws were as amused by Dave's clumsiness in the swamp as he was amazed by their skill there, but Lingle's tone expressed more than mild amusement. Dave said nothing. There would be plenty of fighting soon. He was going to save his breath.

"It's like being back home again, ain't it?" Sarah whispered, half an hour later as she got under the blanket with him. "Don't it seem like getting home again?"

"Well—" said David, who came from Connecticut. "Well, yes and no." Her lithe, young body was warm and vibrant against him. When he turned and took her in his arms she was ready for him, her mouth eager in its soft surrender.

Later he told her: "That world is still out there— that world you haven't seen."

"I got my world right here," she said, holding him close. There was a feeling of contentment, of lassitude in her and it softened her words to a whisper. "I got all the world I want. You came back! I prayed every night

116

that you would, but I didn't really believe it would happen."

"Yes, I came back," David said, suddenly somber.

"Kiss me again," said Sarah. And he did.

CHAPTER 16

HE OUTLINED his plan up in the tower at breakfast.

"New Orleans," Sarah said. "That's South, ain't it? And don't you come from up North? Why do you want to go to New Orleans, mister?"

"My business is there, I've told you."

"Are—are you sure that that's the only reason?"

It was instinct, he saw, that warned her of another woman. It could not have been experience.

"We cross bridges as we come to them," He squeezed her hand. "The first thing is to get clear of this place without being shot."

He rose. Using the glass, he studied the terrain above and below the Brood, noting with relief that there was no sign of smoke. Perhaps he shouldn't have worried. His recruits were not all city ruffians. There were alligator men among them.

"When did you say the shooting starts?"

It was as though she was asking what time he planned to have supper. A spunky girl in the first place, she was so accustomed to bloodshed that she took it for granted. As for that outside world he talked about, her imagination could not encompass it.

"Tomorrow at sunup. We've got to get out before that."

"I ain't any good walking in the woods, mister."

"I'm not either," he said ruefully. "But it's better than just staying here and getting slaughtered."

"Reckon anything's better'n that."

He gazed fondly at Sarah—at her exquisite small head, her tiny mouth, and the straightforward clear hazel eyes, so startling in this resort of shifty smelly men who shuffled or sidled from place to place, chewing, spitting sadly, never looking up. Sarah was clean. She was— what she was. And no fool.

He said, "I wonder if you'll like it out there."

117

She finished her oatmeal and licked the spoon.

"I sure hope I get a chance to find out!" she cried.

The amenities of communal life were never in evidence at Buzzards' Roost. These scoundrels were not sociable. Anything in the way of politeness would have puzzled them, at the same time and by the same token raising their suspicion: for to minds such as theirs, anything not familiar was a thing to be shot at. A "good morning" in this mansion was unheard-of. A grunt would have been thought effusive, any grin an inexcusable spate of sentiment. Dave Macdonough had hardly expected the pirates to gush over him when he came downstairs after his return. He was used to their studied surliness. Nevertheless he sensed that something was wrong. They never had liked him, but they had been afraid of him. He did not think that they were afraid of him now. He took the offensive.

"Damn it, how many times do I have to tell you about that gunpowder? Now sweep it up, and after this keep the door closed!"

They obeyed, muttering, heads down.

"Where else'd we put it?" somebody asked.

"Maybe the wine cellar," Dave said. "I'll take another look."

He did. He was not notably interested in the wine cellar, a large square bricked vault in which it could be assumed that no wine ever had been stored. He'd seen it before, and had been impressed by its size, its dryness, and strength. It might come in handy, he had thought. But just now he was using it only as an excuse to get away. He wanted to collect his thoughts.

Then too, a concern over the loose gunpowder and an effort to find a safer storage space, would argue an interest in the future of Buzzards' Roost. Anyway, Dave hoped they'd take it so.

When he returned to the main hallway he found them there, all eight of them. The gunpowder had been cleaned up but the clearers had not set forth to fish and pot-shot. They stood there. They did not face him —they never did that—but he knew that he was being challenged. He came to a halt.

He said, "Well?"

After a while a Mathewson said something vague about jewelry.

"Oh that!" Dave drew out a long narrow packet of

118

treasury notes wrapped in oiled silk. He slipped the bands off and threw the package on the floor. "Split it up," he said. "I've taken mine."

He went into the magazine. Aside from a natural wish to be armed, he had the thought that an exhibition of marksmanship wouldn't be amiss at just this time. The pirates had always been awed by his pistol shooting. Crack shots themselves with their long Kentucky rifles, they still were somewhat uneasy in the presence of pistols, a gentleman's weapon.

He picked seven or eight guns. He even thought of trying out those Colt's patents, the ones with the revolving chambers, but he gave this up as too dangerous. He filled a flask with powder; cut himself a large chunk of lead; took up a mould, nippers, swabs, a rod; and went back to the hall.

The boys were examining the money, passing it around. "Might've brung gold," Eben muttered.

"And sink to the bottom of the river? There's more than three thousand dollars there. A horse couldn't swim carrying all that in gold."

The sum stunned them. Slow, they had not yet added the figures on the various notes. They kept turning them over and over.

"It don't say what state," Ik said.

"They're good in any state, you fool. Those are federal notes."

He spent the morning and the early part of the afternoon in the tower, blasting at a dipper Sarah had nailed to a tree in the clearing before the house. The container part of this dipper stuck out sideways, and the shots, being downward, plopped harmlessly into earth where there were no stones, precluding the possibility of a ricochet. Every time he hit—and it was a tiny target for that distance—the sound of the shot was followed by a sharp high "ping." There were a good many "pings" that day, as no doubt the pirates noted.

In the middle of the afternoon he lay down with Sarah. "For a rest," he explained. "We're going to need rest. We're going to need all our strength."

How true this was, especially in his own case, he learned a few minutes later when the boys came knocking on the door.

Ordinarily these days, Cateau, who clearly had been in command during Dave's absence, more or less used

119

Jake Lingle as deputy and runner of errands. This time, however, it was not just Jake. It was the whole crew, all eight of them. They looked mighty serious.

"Now what the hell does this mean?" David demanded. "I've told you I don't want to be—"

"We think you better come outside," Cateau said. "There's a man wants to see you."

"A man—"

Fear grabbed David's heart with a cold hand. His mind seethed. Had somebody jumped the gun? His orders had been that Buzzards' Roost was not even to be approached until dawn of the following day. Had one of the hired raiders somehow got lost and stumbled upon this place? Or had one of them deserted? In either case the game would be up and Sarah's life and his own wouldn't be worth so much as a sneeze.

No wonder the boys looked serious.

"I'll be back in a few minutes," Dave called over his shoulder.

"Well, maybe you will and maybe you won't," Cateau muttered.

Dave ignored this. He closed the door.

"Now," he said, "who is this man?"

"Don't know. Never saw him before. But we know who he *says* he is."

"Oh?"

"He *says* he's Captain Flambeau."

A saying has it that he who hesitates is lost. Dave Macdonough did not hesitate. He was used to picking his way among the lightnings, and his step was serene as he went downstairs. To see him, one might have supposed that he greeted pretenders from nowhere every day of the week.

Somehow, even before he reached the veranda, he knew who the man in the front yard was, and for this reason he had no need to sponge astonishment from his face when he confronted Bettlebrow of the bottle-green coat. He did not need to bow, as he might otherwise have done, in order to conceal his confusion.

Beetlebrow, for his part, just as surely recognized Dave. His snake's eyes flashed. His lips, bright red under the mustache, stretched in a thin thorny smile. Beetlebrow's formal name didn't matter. The question of how he had got here, whether by accident or design, seemed equally unimportant. The point was: he *was* here.

Whether as a result of long planning or on the spur of the moment, he was making a bid for the Buzzards' Roost leadership. He had to be met.

The man looked stronger than ever, incalculably strong. His weeks in the wilderness had been hard on him sartorially. His coat was torn in many places, ripped by spiked plants, and so were his trousers and boots, besplattered in addition by mud. His beaver had been dented and scratched, though he still cocked it at an arrogant angle. His face and hands were puffed with mosquito bites. Yet he was a fine physical specimen. He didn't carry an ounce of fat on his frame. He stood firm, alert, ready for anything.

"So you think you're Captain Flambeau," David said.

"I know damn well I'm Captain Flambeau! Who in hell are *you?*"

Argument would be out of place here. Dave could tell the boys of the circumstances in which he had previously met this man, but the boys wouldn't believe, or would not care. The only thing that mattered was the fact that a man had directly defied Dave's authority, the first person to do so since he'd beaten Jake Lingle. Everything hung on this. It was not a time for explanations, which in any case would be lost. It was a time for action.

David, who was being glared at, did not glare. Already he had begun to fight. As Judge Ryerson had pointed out, a duel was much like a game of poker. Right away wasn't too early to start the bluff. A sneer at this stage of the game might be as good as a blow later on. So David seemed cool when he turned, in a manner almost negligent, to Ik Mathewson.

"Fetch some rope," he said.

He addressed himself again to Beetlebrow, and his voice even had a touch of weariness in it.

"We have a place where we hang people who interfere with our business. You may have heard of it. It's called Hogbelly. There are still a few corpses there, I believe, though if a former friend were to come along he'd hardly recognize them in the state they're in now. But there's room for another."

The big man did not bat an eye.

"You are thinking of hanging me?" he asked.

"Only after you're dead."

"You're not going to fight then?"

"Of course, and I'm the one who's going to kill you."

"No," the big man said. "*I'm* going to kill *you*."

Dave shrugged.

"It will be one of us," he promised.

He looked around. He had no choice. He remembered again what Jason Martineau had told him in his hotel room that morning—that your ruler often is a slave of those he rules. He must give them what they want. He can't change the course of events: at best he can only ride along with it on his own terms. These pirates wanted blood. They'd get blood. It was up to him.

"We might as well go now and get it over with," he said. "Jake, you tell Sarah we'll be back by dark. And don't let her get the notion that because there seems to be company she'd better fry more fish. *There will be the same number as usual for supper tonight.*"

He looked at the newcomer. "Come along," he said, and strode off in the direction of Hogbelly Island.

CHAPTER 17

DAVE HAD more than one reason for this quick decision. Fight they must—dickering would only postpone the conflict and perhaps give the newcomer time to get in some psychological licks of his own—so Dave called the turn. They would fight on his terms.

The man with the meeting eyebrows was strong, and surely he was tough, and he was larger than David. But at Hogbelly he would be battling on the ground on which his comrades had been killed, in fact in the very shadow of their dangling remains. No matter how callous he was, this must make some difference to him.

David did not stride into the jungle first. He stepped aside at the edge of the clearing and waved his enemy ahead. Again he had a reason. No alligator man, he was not graceful in the swamp. When he walked there he slid and floundered. He did not want the man he was about to tangle with to see this awkwardness. Besides, being first might bring about in Beetlebrow a feeling of the lamb being led to the slaughter. This David could hope for, anyway. Every little bit helped.

To give Beetlebrow credit, he didn't seem to care

who went first, or how fast. The man showed not an iota of uneasiness, but strode on ahead as though absolutely sure of himself.

When the beach was reached, too, Bettlebrow did not appear even to glance at the five monstrosities that hung still from five tree branches. He immediately took off his hat, coat, waistcoat and boots. He rolled up the sleeves of his shirt.

"Any weapons?" he asked.

"No," Dave said, before anybody else could speak.

"All right."

Dave stripped to the waist. His back to Beetlebrow, he flexed his muscles, tightened his galluses, twisted his bare feet firmly in the slime—bare feet were better than boots in such a spot—and then carefully turned.

The river was on his right. The boys were on his left, hunkered down, their necks craning, eyes bright, all expectancy. Before them, about between Cateau and Ik Mathewson, Dave placed his own bowie knife and a pair of pistols he had been carrying. The pistols—he missed those Ketlands!—were single-barreled Derringers of a very large bore. They were loaded, but not cocked.

He regarded the field. He nodded.

"Ready?" he asked, deigning to look at Beetlebrow for the first time since they had reached this place.

"Any time you are." •

"Good," David said. "Come on."

It will still some time short of sunset, and a steady northern breeze rippled the water. The same breeze stirred the five suspended skeletons, causing them to rattle. That's all they were now—skeletons. Only scraps of clothing clung to them, and they no longer stank. Even the buzzards had given them up.

David walked swiftly toward the man and lashed out right and left, connecting with the right, missing with the left. He hit again for the jaw, and now his right fist stung. It was like pounding a stone wall. He danced back, then immediately went in once more.

He should not have been so precipitate. Beetlebrow caught him in a flying-mare. Beetlebrow's great body swung to one side as easily as might a column of smoke, and David was pitched across the outthrust knee, while a fist like a sledge hammer hit the back of his neck. He thudded hard. Soft though the ground was, it seemed to him then like rock.

123

He twisted just in time. Beetlebrow, with a speed he hadn't expected in such a large man, already was jumping toward him, knees down. Beetlebrow would have used his feet, had he worn boots.

It was a classic maneuver, permissible even under London prize ring rules—and of course *anything* went at Hogbelly.

Beetlebrow's knees met mud. Yet, fast though Dave was, one of those knees glanced off his right side. Dave hardly felt it when he rolled out of reach and sprang to his feet. Upright, however, he knew that he had been hurt. His right side burned as though a fire was there. A split rib? It seemed likely.

He was not breathing hard. He spat. He wiped his mouth with the back of his right hand. He went at Beetlebrow again. And Beetlebrow was up, ready for him.

David knew for sure now that he was in for the fight of his life. Brawn he'd expected, and anticipated. Speed he could cope with. And desperation, to be sure, had been taken for granted. But he had not thought to meet such a high degree of professionalism. That flying-mare had been brilliantly executed.

He would do well to be wary.

For a little while they seesawed, feeling one another out, seldom punching, never closing, each minding his wind, conserving his strength. Dave quickly learned that while the big man's fist landed hard and heavy, his blow was not the bonecrusher that might have been expected. He fought with elbows high, palms in, in the conventional manner, and when he punched they were down-blows, choppy, jolting but not smashing. Dave decided that he could risk them in order to get some of his own to the jaw. The big man never hooked, and Dave was a hooker. The big man relied on fists and elbows and forearms for blocking, and kept his neck stiff, his chin in. Dave, on the other hand, used a constant weaving motion of the body as he went in.

At the same time, the dexterity with which he had performed that flying-mare, the speed with which he'd leapt on David afterward, and now his obvious eagerness to close, all suggested that Beetlebrow, if no great shakes as a boxer, was a master wrestler, an adept of the fall. His greater strength and weight would help him there. If ever they were locked together he could

124

knock the wind out of David and perhaps literally crush him to death in a long terrible bear-hug.

So, as much as he could, Dave stayed away.

Dave's own punches, with everything he had behind them, seemed not to bother the big man at all. Dave's hands hurt. His right side was a great flame of pain now.

This went on for some time, the big man trying to close, David staying away. Neither of them said anything, or grinned, or scowled. They were serious about the business. The play-acting was over now.

It was Dave who brought about the break. He was sweating very little. He wasn't winded, and his head was clear, for he'd scarcely been hit. His right side was a great agony, but he could grit his teeth against that. What started to go first, one by one, twanging, were his nerves. He felt that he *had* to knock that man down! The lack of expression on Beetlebrow's big face, his imperturbability, like his refusal to duck, his calm acceptance of blows he could not block, began to drive David wild.

He got too near. Pressing it, he swung too wide. His right foot slipped. He was only off-balance for an instant, but Beetlebrow, who must have been waiting for something like this, needed no more.

Dave felt his left forearm grasped. He was not yanked into that bear-hug he had feared and which instinctively he started to resist, but instead was *snapped* as the end boy in a game of snap-the-whip is snapped. Helpless as a stuffed doll, he was literally hurled half the length of the clearing.

He landed hard, perhaps thirty feet from Beetlebrow. But the big man was jumping even before Dave struck. Dave saw him coming and tried to roll away. But the big man fell on him, knees first.

The next minute was a blur to Dave Macdonough. He was not fighting as much as he was squirming, trying to wriggle out from under, trying to protect his throat, his groin.

It was like being in a vise. He was completely covered, and every move he made was blocked. All the while the pressure increased. His ears were ringing. His heart beat wildly. He could hardly breathe.

He never did know to what he owed his release. Suddenly he found himself free—that was all. Beetlebrow

125

perhaps had been shifting his grip, preparatory to the final squeeze? Whatever it was, Beetlebrow recovered quickly and tried to pin Dave down again, but Dave rolled clear.

Dave got to his feet. The world rocked. Attacked then, he would have been helpless, as easy to knock down as a rotten fence post. But Beetlebrow was in no position to attack. Beetlebrow was rising slowly, not springing up. So *he* too was feeling it? Not all of those punches had gone to waste!

Dave nodded thoughtfully, panting. He raised his swollen fists.

So it was that he and his mortal enemy again stood face to face, and the world was not rocking so erratically now. Squatting, silent, hot-eyed, the boys watched.

The buzzards came back. Each with a loud "whoosh" of its wings, settled along the bank of the river, facing in. Each watched in silence, its head thrust forward.

The scene then was macabre. On one side, the hunched attentive pirates of the Roost; on the other, lined up like a chorus, equally intent, the buzzards.

The buzzards knew what they were about. They'd get one of these men. Which one? It was only a matter of waiting. The buzzards had plenty of time.

Dave licked his lips. Every breath he took drew a knife into his side. Nevertheless, and for the first time, he began to grin. He shook his head. He moved in.

Where he found the strength he didn't know. He was a slugging machine now, nothing less. He had no thought and no feeling. All he knew were that hard heavy pale face, those eyes of a snake, the cruel dark mouth. He kept hitting that mouth.

So Beetlebrow was feeling them, eh? Well, Beetlebrow would get more.

Dave could go down this way, swinging punches. He supposed he could die this way. He didn't care.

But it was the big man who went down. He didn't crash, spread-eagling his arms. He did not fall like an oak that's been axed. Rather, he crumpled. His legs gave. He started to fold up, jerkily, like some curious, stiff, mechanical toy.

Suspicious, smelling a trick, and scarcely able to stand up anyway, Dave stepped back.

Beetlebrow went to his knees. His arms, the arms of an ape, hung limp at his sides. He swayed. Head bowed, a grotesque figure, he might have been offering up a prayer to the gods of the swampland.

David took a deep breath—and almost screamed in pain. Now was the time to finish the job. Now was the moment he dreaded.

Cateau reached out a hand that was like a claw, and sent one of the Derringers spinning across to Beetlebrow, It came to rest right in front of the man.

When he did this Cateau must have supposed that David Macdonough couldn't see. Perhaps Dave looked unconscious, his eyes glazed, even as he stood there.

Cateau had not done it impulsively, without stopping to think. Cateau was not an impulsive man.

Beetlebrow saw the thing. He could hardly help but see it, if he had any sight left at all. It was his one chance, that pistol. He gave a low glad cry, a sort of gurgle, and reached down and grasped the thing. He could hardly be blamed for this. Those buzzards weren't waiting there for nothing.

David sprang.

The big man was rising, dazed, the pistol held before him muzzle-up, his finger not yet having found the trigger, when David reached him. The man tried to bring the muzzle down. David tried to force it up.

Away from the pirates they reeled, close together, swaying, sobbing.

The pistol went off.

David thought he was dead. He truly believed so, for a moment. The world blotted out, smoke stung his eyes, a wave of heat seared up his chest and past his face. Oddly, he was never conscious of the *noise* of the explosion, which must have been stunning. To David it all seemed to be happening in a vacuum.

Beetlebrow went down. He no longer had a face. The ball might have gone up through his throat and into his brain, but even if there had been no ball at all the powder would have burned him to death. He'd received the full force of it. His neck was torn open. His mouth and nose, almost literally ripped off, were black, like all the rest of the front of his head excepting the eyes, which, seeing nothing, bugged out like those of a squashed frog.

A neat round cloud of smoke, looking like a white silk sofacushion miraculously afloat, or a trim white silk balloon, hung motionless above the clearing. Then the breeze found it—the same breeze that made the skeletons rattle and clack—and carried it primly away.

David looked at the weapon in his hand. It still smoked.

He looked at Cateau, who had not stirred. He went to Cateau. The man's face was dead-pale, but still he did not move.

David threw the empty pistol into his face. The rear sight cut his left cheek, which began to bleed.

"I've done enough killing for today," David said. "We'll settle this later."

He started back toward Sarah.

CHAPTER 18

THAT NIGHT there was a small cold moon the color of a lemon, somewhat that shape too. It tossed bright planes of light through the windows and onto the floor—stripes, bars, squares. Almost with the solemnity of superstition, like a child who refrains from stepping on cracks, Sarah and David circled these planes, sticking to the dark, as they went downstairs.

At the floor of the main staircase, carelessly, as if tossed there, lay one of the boys. It was impossible to tell which. Certainly, however, he was not a sentry. The boys habitually slept anywhere their fancy suggested —most often, if the wind was right and it wasn't raining, on the veranda. The fact that this one was sleeping here meant nothing—except that they'd have to step over him. He was twitching, no doubt tormented by a dream, and his breathing suggested a stabbed fish.

Their plan, discussed in whispers hours ago, was to pass through the kitchen and slip out by way of the back door. Then they would go to the privy, one by one, without haste. The idea was that if anybody happened to glance out a back window and see a person making for that ramshackle little building, he would attach no importance to it. To be sure, if he continued to watch the privy and saw *another* person go there, the first not yet having returned, he might fall to wondering about this—might even investigate. This was not likely to happen. The denizens of Buzzards' Roost were

troubled by hookworm, dandruff, acne, boils, caries, lice
—but not by insomnia.

From the privy it was only a few feet to the shadows
of the swamp itself. If they were seen during the dash,
and an alarm was raised, they were lost. The boys, cats
in the dark, would surround and slaughter them. On the
other hand, if they could get a start there seemed no
reason why they should not find their way to the river.
To be sure, among the islands of Satan's Brood the
mighty Mississippi's channel sometimes seemed no more
than a back-country creek; but it was certain that *any* running water they came upon would be some part of the
river, and of course they could tell which way it ran,
whatever the darkness, merely by feeling it with their
hands. Then they could make their way upstream along
the bank, and sooner or later they were almost certain
to come to Hogbelly, which was near the northern end
of the channel.

Even before they got to Hogbelly they might en-
counter one of Dave's converging squads. Sarah, in case
they were separated, knew the password.

So now they stepped over the snorer at the foot of
the stairs, Dave going first with his longer legs, to help
Sarah afterward. The sleeper only continued to twitch
and snort.

At the back door they stopped in dismay.

Seated on a stump about halfway to the little out-
building was Ik Mathewson. He wasn't doing anything
—just probing his left ear with a toothpick and staring
noncommittally at the moon.

Again there was nothing to indicate that Ik was a
sentry. Nevertheless, there the man sat.

They waited a long time—they couldn't know how
long—before the Doorknob slowly rose, still twisting the
toothpick in his ear, and spat, and stretched, and
started for the house. They flattened themselves on
either side of the back door, and he passed within inches
of them. They heard him go to the veranda, heard him
flop down.

They waited a little longer, as long as they could
trust their nerves, and then they went ahead as planned,
one by one, slowly, Sarah first.

Nothing happened. There was no alarm.

In the privy, standing, holding hands, straining their
ears, they waited again for as long as they dared.

Then, side by side, they ran for it.

The swamp loomed like a solid wall. They raised their arms before their faces, and it was hard to keep on running even then. Their tense muscles cried out against the deed. But they did it.

Now, abruptly, they were immersed. It had been like diving into dark water. Not able to see each other, holding hands, slipping, stumbling, letting go, scrambling up, they reached out piteously. They were scared. When their contact broke momentarily, they knew panic.

Even with Sarah sharing the predicament, side by side, Dave had never before felt so horribly *alone*. It was as though he had been projected hundreds of thousands of years back in time, so that now he floundered through primordial ooze, hemmed in by wet vegetation and by monsters he couldn't see, while nobody in heaven above or on the earth beneath could help him.

Moonlight had been bad enough. This was worse. No glint got through the tangle overhead. He and Sarah moved fitfully, by sound and by feel.

After a while they stopped, ashamed of themselves, and kissed, and held on to one another, panting. For it was close in the swamp, where the air was steamy, so that it was not easy to catch your breath.

Sarah sagged. Dave tried to hold her by one elbow while he waved downward with his other hand, turning in an effort to find a place for her to sit. Everything he touched was wet and sticky and soft.

"I'm all right," she gasped. "Let's go on."

Now they were steadier, yet they trembled still. To move took a terrible effort. Low branches stabbed them. Tree roots, arching themselves out of the muck as though in agony, tripped them. Time and again they fell to hands and knees. Creepers and vines that dangled from the unseen trees caught them with thorns, scratching them, tearing their clothes.

They could not see what was underfoot. Sometimes they splashed through water, once almost up to their knees.

Worst of all was the Spanish moss. They were never clear of its fingers, which were wet, spongy, tomb-cold, forever slyly brushing their faces.

They hoped they were headed for the river bank somewhere near the spot where on two occasions Dave had landed from a steamer. They had, as they supposed, carefully half-circled the mansion. They should now be going slightly downhill. But since they seldom took an unobstructed step it was impossible to be sure of this. They might, for all they knew, be going *up*hill.

At last they came to a fallen tree—they banged into it—and stopped, sitting down. The tree was crumbly, half rotten, but still the most substantial thing they had come upon.

They sat panting, holding one another tight.

What time was it? They had no way of knowing. Sarah never had been permitted to examine the stolen articles cached at Buzzards' Roost, and didn't know how to tell time anyway. David had no watch of his own.

Wise in this at least, the boys had seen to it that no defined path was made between the mansion and the river. David, who had been over the route only a few times, only twice in the daytime, could remember no landmark. Sarah was afraid of the swamp, and in her four years at the Roost she had never strayed more than a few hundred yards away. Neither had she ever overheard anything that might help them now.

"We'll get you there," he whispered, as though the outside world was a definite point-at-able place, a dock, a platform. "We'll make it yet, somehow."

She did not say anything. She just clung to him.

There was a sound behind them, a sort of grunt.

They sprang to their feet, whirling around, hearts beating wildly, and David drew a pistol.

"Who's that?" he whispered.

"T-Tuscaloosa," Sarah ventured the signal.

There was a slight yet somehow large sound a few feet in front of them. It was a watery sound, a sort of splash, followed by silence.

It took all their resolve to keep from running.

"You reckon it was a 'gator?" Dave asked at last.

"Must have been. Couldn't be anything else."

They did not go straight as they had planned after that, but tried to give the place the sound had come from a wide berth. It made them shiver when they had to slosh through water, and they hurried, no longer afraid to splash. A beast like that, swimming unheard, could snap off your leg.

Three times they came upon columns of moonlight, each of which stamped out a body of water the way a cookie-cutter cuts out a cookie. The water in each case

131

was stagnant, scummy. The tiny patch of sky above told nothing.

Again and again they stopped dead in their tracks and strained their ears, hoping to hear something—a steamboat whistle, anything—that would give them an idea of the direction of the river.

Dave decided to climb a tree. Sarah was terrified at the prospect of being alone even for a little while, but he soothed her, quieting her fears. He picked a big tree, his thought being that if he could climb to the top he might glimpse the river.

The tree that he selected was big-around, which is why he supposed that it was tall. He had no other way of telling. Presumably the lower branches of a tall tree would be high above the ground, and he knew from experience that the Spanish moss would come off in huge hanks. He did not count on this but on the lianas, if that's what they were—creepers, parasitic vines of some sort—in which every tree hereabouts seemed smothered. He tested several of these, which were like stiff clumsy ropes. One seemed to hold. He started up it, hand-over-hand.

He did not get far. As the vine loosened in his hand with jerky cushioned jolts, he grabbed others. They too gave way, and when he tumbled the few feet to the ground he carried great masses of them with him.

He tried twice more to climb that tree, and once tried to climb another. The result was the same each time. Nothing in all this sink of rottenness and gluey goo, it would seem, had any real substance. Nothing was firm. Everything gave.

Bruised, baffled, he quit.

At the edge of the third tarn or pool they came upon, they lay down, exhausted. They could find no dry place, nor even a place that was tolerably level. They lay in the mud, too tired to care.

Dave made a pillow of his coat, and they clung together, not in passion now, but in shivering fear.

They must have slept. When next Dave looked at the patch of sky he saw that the moon had set, while the stars looked washed, paling.

"We'd better keep moving," he whispered.

"Y-yes."

They were chilled through, all their clothes wet. Fumbling, they could scarcely feel one another, their hands were so cold.

Dave had difficulty pulling his folded coat out of the mire, so deeply had it become imbedded. It stank of stagnant water. He would not have put it back on, except that he was afraid of catching a crippling ague.

Obviously they had to walk. If they didn't walk they might die. The swamp was insidious. It sought now to lull them. They had a suicidal desire to lie down and just let everything go. It was a fight even to get to their feet. They trudged on, stumbling, sobbing.

For a little while David carried Sarah, holding her close to him so she would catch the warmth of his body. He had to give this up because he fell asprawl, time after time. With his burden, he couldn't put out his hands to break these falls, and they hurt Sarah more than they hurt him. She whimpered, insisting on being let down.

"*Something's* got to happen soon," he puffed. "We've got to get *somewhere!*"

They did. A few minutes after he had spoken—the first thing either had said in a long while—they detected a filmy light ahead. It was hardly more than that, yet it might mark a clearing, or even the river.

It was a clearing all right. They burst into it.

A few hundred feet away, facing them, was a large unpainted three-story house with a square tower on top.

They were standing on the very spot where David had fought Jake. They had moved in a complete circle.

Jake himself was up there on the veranda, in company of the other boys, who lounged about, some cleaning their rifles, some dippering whisky out of the barrel.

"Have a nice walk?" Lingle asked.

CHAPTER 19

THEY crossed the veranda amid a stunning silence, and the men fell in behind them.

They stood in the middle of the big downstairs hall, uncertain what to do—for Ik Mathewson lounged in the doorway of the kitchen, where Sarah would ordinarily go, while at the foot of the stairs, Cateau sat honing his knife.

Again the floor was streaked with rivulets of gunpowder, crisscrossed with them. Dave said nothing. Cursing them for their sloppiness was a worn-out evasion.

He turned. The boys were all there. They were even venturing to look at him now.

His heart sank. He knew that bluster wouldn't help any longer. The end had come. The feet of clay had been discovered. The idol was about to be smashed.

"Well?" he said.

Flies hummed around the fishheads on the floor. The sound of Cateau's knife along the stone was thin, slaty.

"We thought you better come outside and talk this over," Jake Lingle said.

"Talk what over?"

"You better come."

No doubt he could get one of them. He might even get two. But there were eight.

Sarah flew at Jake, spitting.

"What are you going to do with him?"

Jake fended her off. He looked at her.

"Shut up," he said at last.

"You better worry about what we're going to do to *you*, afterward," Cateau said, honing his knife.

Dave took her shoulders from behind. He lowered his head.

"Try to make a dash for it out back, after we've gone."

"No."

"Tut, tut." He shook her gently, even lovingly. He gave her a small shove toward the kitchen. "There's a girl now. Make me some coffee. I'll be back in a few minutes."

Cateau sniggered.

Dave straightened his cravat. He took off his beaver and sleeved it and put it back on. He tugged down his coat. "All right, you louts. Where do we have this conference?"

"You'll find out soon enough. Come on."

Five of them went ahead of him to the veranda. The others, Ik Mathewson, Cateau and Jake Lingle, closed in behind. They knew he had pistols, and they were taking no chances.

The sun was up now, streaming into the clearing slantwise from behind the house. This left the veranda still somewhat dim—a fact which undoubtedly saved David Macdonough's life.

134

As Dave stepped over the threshold, a terrific explosion issued from the swamp. A cloud of smoke rose.

The man just ahead of Dave slammed back as though axed in the chest. Dave ducked trying to hold him up as a shield. But he was a dead weight and bigger than Dave, and he slithered to the floor. Twisting, crouching, Dave dived for the doorway through which he had just come. There was a "click" near his left ear, and suddenly that side of his face burned as though from fire. Flying splinters had caught him. Inside, on the floor, he rolled. The explosion in the swamp continued like a long peal of thunder. Dirty white smoke rolled. The air whined with balls. Dust jigged. Chunks of plaster began to fall out of the walls and ceiling.

Dave tossed a glance at Sarah. She had not lost her head. She might have tried to dash out by the back way, but she remembered what Dave said, and sensibly she stayed.

Dave looked slantwise through the doorway. He saw a man get to hands and knees. There were more shots, and the man collapsed.

Eben Mathewson, who had perhaps been playing 'possum, now sprang to his feet and ran for the doorway. He made it, but not alive. At the threshold he lurched as if kicked from behind. His back arched, he was shoved halfway across the hall, and he fell on his face. Blood began to stain the back of his shirt in five or six places.

"They sure got plenty of lead," Jake Lingle muttered.

Jake cautiously approached a window. Ik Mathewson, without a sob for his brother, wriggled on his belly toward the door, pushing his rifle ahead of him. Cateau left the stairs and snaked out through the kitchen, doubtless to see if he could draw fire in the rear.

It was Dave's chance. He looked at Sarah, swiveled his eyes toward the stairway, and nodded. They ran.

Nobody shouted. So far as they knew they were not even missed. Dave peeled his coat off as he ran up one flight of steps after another. "Worth trying anyway," he called. "When we get there, yell 'Tuscaloosa!' for all you're worth!"

He had shucked coat and vest like a cornhusk and began ripping off his shirt as they reached the trapdoor leading up to the tower.

"Tuscaloosa! Tuscaloosa!"

"*Keep down!*" Dave yelled. "*Flat down!*"

135

"Tuscaloosa! Don't shoot!"

Dave knelt below one of the windows. He raised the shirt, started to wave it.

The gunfire had never ceased, but now it was no longer a continuous roar, being rather an intermittent spat-spat-spat-spat. There was an extra burst when the shirt went up, and Dave hastily lowered it.

"You picked good ones," Sarah said, squatting beside him.

He made a wry smile as he examined the shirt. It had four holes in it.

The spat-spat-spat-spat went on. Dave deduced that the deputies were firing into the bodies on the veranda, just to make sure that none still lived. Sometimes there would be a shot from the house.

"Yes, I picked good ones all right. That's their orders —nobody leaves here alive."

Sarah rolled her eyes.

"At that, it's better'n being in the swamp," she whispered. "Think they'll rush the house?"

"I doubt it. Why should they?"

"They got food?"

"Enough for four days."

"*We* haven't," she pointed out.

"No, but I figure that when the shooting lets up a bit we can maybe make ourselves heard. After all, I'm their paymaster."

"The boys downstairs'd hear it too. It'd gravel them no end."

"Well, I wouldn't expect it to make 'em happy."

"They might come busting up here after us."

Dave touched his pistols.

"They can only come one by one, and I can handle 'em that way. Meanwhile we'll close this—"

He crawled to the trapdoor, but he did not close it. Kneeling, bending over the opening, he started to sniff, to shake his head.

"Come here. See if you smell this."

She did.

"*Smoke!*"

He nodded, pop-eyed. He swung his legs over, clambered down the ladder, made for the staircase. From there he could see past the second floor and almost to the first. The smoke was coming from the first floor,

136

from the main hallway, near the powder magazine. And there was a lot of it, more all the time.

He ran down the stairs.

What had started the fire, Dave wondered despairingly as he ran. A flashback perhaps: some of the boys still carried rifles with flintlock firing fixtures instead of the more modern nipple-and-percussion-cap apparatus. It didn't matter. The hall was a mass of flames.

These were not large tonguelike flames. Small, swift, perky, they scurried here and there with the brisk inanity of ants.

The newel post at the foot of the stairs had become ignited, as had the baseboard of the wall at several points, but the blaze at those points was languid and could have been put out with ease. It was not so with the gunpowder fire—or fires. The extent of the spillage now became hideously apparent. Since the black grains had mixed with the dust of the floor they were not conspicuous to the casual eye; but the fire found them out and pursued them this way and that. The floor was alive with these swift streakings of flame. And every one of them, though it might zigzag erratically for a while, in the end moved straight for the place from whence the powder had come —the magazine.

Daylight, still dim, drizzled in through the open doorway, while the figures of Ik, Jake and the agile Cateau, as they hopped and stamped, waving their arms and gibbering, suggested those of imps.

Smoke swirled, and the dust dancing in the air was reddened by the gleam.

In the middle of the hall lay the body of Eben Mathewson. A snake of small flames, skittering past, had touched the trousers and set them afire. Dry, they burned stodgily.

All this Dave saw in the blink of an eye as he ran down the stairs. An instant later he was among the others, stamping, swearing, leaping from place to place. He blinked in the acrid air. He too was an imp now, grimacing, convulsive, an inhabitant of Hell.

"Don't get near that door!"

They did not have to tell him this. Commanded by the sharpshooters of the swamp, the doorway meant death. Fortunately it was on the far side of the hall, away from the fire.

The alligator men had calloused feet, and David's

boots were strong. The trouble was, while sometimes when they stamped on a series of small flames they would put it out, at other times they'd only scatter it. The flames had a fondness for the cracks of the floor, where gunpowder had been accumulating for months, and as they raced along these they were especially hard to put out.

Dave collided with Jake Lingle. It was purely an accident, but Jake, sweating, weeping, cursing, seemed to take it as an insult. He let out a roar of rage:

"You're the one brought 'em! You brought 'em here!"

His rifle had been tossed aside, but now he fetched out his bowie knife. He held it point-up, like a sword. He started for Dave.

"Never mind that now," Dave said.

Jake came on in, bending low. His eyes were wild.

"Stop it," Dave cried, working a pistol out of his pocket.

Jake sprang. Dave shot him in the shoulder, and he spun clear around and sprawled beside the body of Eben Mathewson. His trousers caught fire from Mathewson's and they too sent out a lot of low smudgy smoke.

Dave Macdonough had gone back to stamping even before Jake hit the floor. There was no time to be lost.

Now, whether because of somebody's feet or because of a vagrant breeze, instead of a serpent of fire there was a puff of it, a fan, outspreading. It was within a few feet of the door of the gunpowder room, a door that fitted badly. A horizontal sheet of flame, it moved fast.

They all saw it at the same time. Each of them was several yards away.

Cateau threw himself into a corner, his arms over his head, waiting for the explosion.

Ik Mathewson ran for the veranda. Whether he forgot, in his panic, or whether he was deliberately choosing death in this form, nobody would ever know. Arms spread, bellowing like a bull, he charged through the doorway. He was immediately hit, but he surged on, a man in a frenzy, pausing only for a split second each time a ball found him, until at last he pitched head-first down the veranda steps and to the ground. The boys in the jungle, seeking to make sure of the job, kept firing into his body.

Dave started for the fire, inches now from the wide slit under the door.

He could never have reached it in time. Sarah got there first. Sarah had followed him downstairs, and now

138

she hurled herself full-length across the fan of small fires, smothering it. The burlap sacking that was her garment began to spit and spark. She gave a low moan. Dave ran to her.

"*Hold it!*"

Cateau had come to his feet again, and Cateau meant fight. The hysteria had gone out of him. He was cold now, a killer. What happened to Sarah—whether she burned to death—did not in the least concern him. He no longer even feared the fire. A maniac with a will of ice, he had one thought only—to murder David Macdonough.

Cateau had waited a long while for this moment. His eyes glittered. His mouth worked, and there was a shiny spot of spit at each end of it.

He held a horse pistol at his hip.

"You fool!" Dave shouted. "Can't you see—"

Cateau fired.

The echoes of the shot banged back and forth, while through them could be heard the dribble of plaster out of a hole that appeared in the wall behind Dave.

Cateau dropped the pistol. He drew his bowie knife.

Dave drew his only loaded pistol, pointed it, pulled the trigger. There was a sharp click, nothing more.

A defective cap? He thumbed the striker back, pulled again. A click.

Cateau grinned. He began to shuffle in, crouching, his hands hanging almost to the floor, the knife point-forward ahead of him.

Dave drew his own bowie.

Now here Cateau had all the advantage. David Macdonough never had been a knife fighter, whereas this was the weapon the alligator man knew best. Moreover, in such a clash skill was of supreme importance, technique told the tale. Reach counted for little, strength for less. It was a matter of knowing what to do and just when to do it—a matter of timing. That, and speed.

The wily Cateau, then, was perfectly at home. The blade he had sharpened beside half a hundred campfires, the blade he loved, was in his fist. His enemy was before him. He shuffled in, seemingly awkward, in fact a fiend of slaughterous efficiency.

Dave felt a cold hand enclose his heart, squeezing it. Nevertheless he did not wait for Cateau to come, but went to meet the man.

Cateau lunged low on the left, after having feinted

139

right. Dave was not to be taken in by such a trick. He twisted his body to the lunge, causing it to miss his ribs by inches, and he slashed down at Cateau's wrist. Cateau was almost unbelievably quick—a wraith rather than a mortal, material man. It was like stabbing at smoke. He had recovered with the speed of lightning, and was back in place, leering a little, unbloodied, but wary now.

Dave went at him.

Dave was overeager. He was not concentrating as he should have done, for part of his mind was on Sarah, who lay moaning. His cut was fast, but not fast enough. And Cateau, prepared for such precipitancy, didn't give him time to get back. Cateau slammed down Dave's knife hand, his left fist hammering the top of Dave's right wrist, and he closed.

Warned perhaps by some atavistic instinct, Dave half-turned. That saved his life. Pain seared his left side, shooting clear up to the armpit, but it didn't weaken him. He brought down his left elbow, striving to trap Cateau's knife hand. Cateau yanked back, pulling Dave with him. He was leaning very low, his shoulder against the top of Dave's knife hand.

Now they were exposed to the men outside, and there was an angry splatter of shots. Bullets like bees hummed a horrid chorus through the doorway. The wall, already stippled with holes, became a cloud of plaster motes.

Cateau got free. Dave sprang toward him, but slipped and went to one knee. Dave was forced to put his hands to the floor for an instant; otherwise he would have fallen on his face. Screaming with delight, knife held high, Cateau jumped at him.

That scream was cut short. In his frenzy, carried away by joy, Cateau never knew what hit him. Pushed by a rifle ball that must have caught him squarely in the spine, he fell—was pitched, rather—not upon Dave, but clear over Dave. He died before he landed.

Dave paid him no mind but ran at once to Sarah. He turned her over. She was horribly burned, her face blackened, half the hair singed off her head. Her eyes were glassy. He could not tell whether she recognized him.

He had no sooner moved her than a spurt of flame darted out from under her body, precisely as an insect might dart out from under a stone that you've stirred. Dave, on his knees now, reached out to slap it. He was

140

too late. The flame wriggled right underneath the door and was gone.

Two other strips of flame, racing along two cracks, followed right behind it.

There could be no doubt of what was about to happen.

Dave scooped the girl up in his arms. His left side all wet and sticky now, while the blood even crawled its warm way down into his trousers, he ran under the stairway, kicked open a door, half-ran and half-fell down the narrow steps, and found the wine vault. It was dark there, but dry. He deposited Sarah on the floor, closed the steel door, and went back to her, finding her by means of outstretched hands.

Again she moaned, on a lower note this time.

"Is—is the house going to fall on us, mister?"

"It might, Sarah."

He could not see her. Tears filled his eyes as he thought of that scorched face.

"I'm afraid I ain't ever going to get outside, the way you wanted me to," she whispered. "I—I'm sorry."

"Don't think about it now."

"Maybe it's just as well. Maybe I wouldn't have been able to learn how to be a lady, and then you'd've been ashamed of me."

"Sarah!"

"This is better, mister. Hold me tight—"

At that moment the world seemed to come to an end. The sound of the explosion did not seem great, but its impact was terrific. To Dave, crouching in the darkness below, holding his darling, it was as though the air pressure had suddenly been trebled, so that his eyes hurt horribly, his ears rang, the very guts in his belly felt as though squeezed into a smaller space.

Almost a minute passed before he could breathe again. His heart thudded wildly.

"Reckon the house didn't fall on us after all," he gasped.

There was no answer.

"Sarah, did you hear me?"

The burden he could not even see was limp in his arms. He called to her again and again. He kissed her, shook her.

"*Sarah!*" he cried. And then he gave up and just waited.

It was mid-afternoon before the wreckers reached the cellar. They would never have dug their way there at

141

all had it not been for the absence of the man who had recruited them, Macdonough, the mysterious Yankee who would never say where he came from. *He* might appear at any time, they calculated, and they sought to garner all the loot they could before he did. The pickings were poor enough at best. The cellar seemed a possible hiding place for treasure.

"Not much left of some of 'em," they reported. "Hardly enough to get hung."

Buzzards circled the clearing slowly, awkwardly, low. Their heads were thrust out, their skinny necks taut.

"Hang them anyway," Dave said, "down by the shore, where I told you. You've got plenty of rope."

"Sure—oh, sure."

"Yes, you've got plenty of rope. But for this one—" Dave turned back into the vault—"I want a shovel."

He buried Sarah in the front yard of the black pile of what had once been Buzzards' Roost, while the deputies were busy with the bodies below. From the wreckage they had found beams with which to rig a gallows where all who passed could see. David, using the same source, rigged only a small white cross. He charcoaled her name on this—SARAH. He did not know her last name. She had never known it herself.

He knelt there and prayed for a long while, before that cross. Sarah. The girl who never got outside.

CHAPTER 20

DAVE pocketed the ten thousand dollars. It was largely in fifties, a mighty wad. He cleared his throat.

"Thank you," he said. "You've been fair, and I have an apology to make. When I first came to New Orleans I got the notion that it was run by a lot of stiff-necked aristocrats. I was wrong. You're aristocrats all right, but anybody who thinks you're stiff-necked is crazy. You've acted like folks with me, and I want you to know that I appreciate it."

There was a murmur of applause. Cigar smoke hung in the air. Brandy shone like amber in the exquisitely cut carafes. Mr. Martineau's guests, around the library table, were genially attentive.

"You understand, Mr. Macdonough, that this isn't any common *policeman's* job we're offering you," one of them said. "We want your name, yes. We expect that any company you're connected with isn't going to have much trouble with gamblers and thieves. But we're not paying a fancy salary just for that. This position carries a great deal of responsibility."

"I understand that," David said.

"And under the circumstances we feel that before you accept this handsome offer it might be advisable if you'd sort of fill us in a little on your background. I mean—where you came from and how you happened to get to this part of the world and so-forth. You can see how, naturally, we'd want this information."

"Yes," David said, "I can understand that too."

He reached for his hat, a new one.

"You've been mighty kind and mighty thoughtful," he said. "Now I think I'll go."

"You mean you're going back to your hotel?"

"I mean I'm going to California."

Astounded, as one man they leaned forward.

"*California?* Good God, man, why *California?*"

"There are gold fields there," Dave pointed out.

"But look what we're offering you!" Judge Ryerson said. "And there'd be more coming all the time. There's a heap of money to be made in the steamboating business these days. More'n you'd ever find in California."

"It isn't the gold I'll be going for, really," Dave said.

They stared at him. But Jason Martineau, though a banker, had a dash of the diplomat in him. He rose and went to Dave, and put a hand on Dave's shoulder.

"Look, lad. Come over here, by this door."

He opened the door, having placed Dave so that he faced out.

"Never mind what *we* think," Martineau said in a low voice. "But there's somebody out there who sure wants you to stay in New Orleans, David."

Fireflies flickered. There was no moon. The salmon-colored hibiscus and the Cherokee roses, half closed now, gleamed faintly. The air was heavy with the fragrance of jasmine. From beyond the fence came the subdued rattle of Bourbon Street, a friendly familiar sound. In the drawing room, somebody was playing Chopin.

Adoree Sanderson wore white, and David saw brilliants in her piled hair. Her chin was tipped a little high,

143

as her lips were a little open, and she had clasped her hands before her while she stood by the side of the sun-dial, alone. It was a position curiously suggestive of expectancy. The girl was waiting for something—or some-body. She stood straight, the silk of her frock shimmering softly in the starlight. She had never looked lovelier.

"Hadn't you better talk it over with her, David?"

Dave Macdonough shook his head.

"No, I hadn't," he said slowly. "She's one of you. She'd ask questions. And she'd be entitled to have them an-swered, if I stayed here."

He turned back to the men at the table. He bowed, his hat over his heart, very serious.

"I thought when I started west, gentlemen, that I'd soon find a place where folks didn't ask so many ques-tions about who you are and where you came from. Understand, I'm not blaming you one bit. You've got every right to ask. But—well, I guess it's just that I haven't gone far enough. So I'm going farther. Thank you again, from the bottom of my heart—and good-bye."

He closed the door so quietly behind him that the cigar smoke scarcely swirled, and in a moment it was as though he had never been there.

The money men looked at one another.

After a long while Judge Ryerson reached for his brandy.

"Well now, by God, whatever else you might think of him, gentlemen, there goes a *man!*"

He drank.

THE END